FORBIDDEN BY TIME

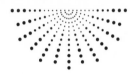

NEGEEN PAPEHN

CITY OWL
PRESS

FORBIDDEN BY TIME
Forbidden Love, Book 3

CITY OWL PRESS
www.cityowlpress.com

Cover Design by Mibl Art and Tina Moss. All stock photos licensed appropriately.

Edited by Yelena Casale.

For information on subsidiary rights, please contact the publisher at info@cityowlpress.com.

Print Edition ISBN: 978-1-949090-41-3

Digital Edition ISBN: 978-1-949090-42-0

Printed in the United States of America

PRAISE FOR NEGEEN PAPEHN

"Forbidden by Faith shows how family, love, and faith can collide, even in this modern age." – *Romance Author, A. K. Leigh*

"Forbidden by Faith is a New Adult coming of age story with several twists, giving us a modern Romeo and Juliet tale where religion, culture, and class prejudice act as the hurdles for our lovers to overcome." – *Romance Author, Katie O' Sullivan*

"A heartfelt immigrant love story." – *Publisher's Weekly*

"Rich in culture, this first book in the Forbidden Love series immediately draws the reader in to this modern take on a familiar star-crossed lovers tale. The chemistry between Sara and Maziar sparks white hot immediately and every interaction sizzles." – *InD'tale*

"Nothing is better than this feeling, when you read the first pages of a book and you just know it will consume you. What I love the most about Papehn is the fact that you can tell that each of the books of this series is written with passion and that it's not just another book to sell to eager readers. Her stories are never predictable, she writes about heavy subjects and it's not always easy to read but it's also never gratuitous, everything on her characters journeys happen for a reason." – *Alyssa of LoveLysBooks*

"Ms. Papehn is a wonderful storyteller! I was immediately caught up in the lives of her characters. In Forbidden by Destiny, the heroine, Leyla, might be of Iranian descent but her story belongs to all women." – *Carrie Nichols, Author of The Small-Town Sweethearts series*

"This book goes far beyond being a romance novel...it covers a range of experiences women might have and treats them in a compassionate, loving, healing way. You're going to want to read this book, I guarantee it, and then you'll want to pass it along to a friend, a sister, or a mother." – *Diane Byington, Author of Who She Is*

For Mike

CHAPTER ONE

If there were pictures in the dictionary, Mom's face would be next to the word *swoon*. The giddy expression she wears every time Maziar and Sara are around resembles that of a lovesick teenager. It wouldn't be so annoying if it weren't always peppered with pitying glances in my direction and covert comments about how I'm not married as well. *Not as hidden as you think, Mom.*

The older sibling left behind in the marital race is an Iranian nightmare. Now add the fact that I'm a girl and you have the perfect recipe for disaster. I should get used to it. I can only assume if Mom looks at me this way, everyone else is probably saying worse. The lack of a husband when currently of childbearing age is not a cute accessory.

You'd think, at twenty-eight, I would still have lots of time, but Persian girl years resemble that of dogs—for every one we get older, we age a decade. I'm officially approaching old maid status. Ridiculous, but sadly the truth of it. I'm not vying to get married or anything. Or maybe I am, but that's just what I tell myself. I honestly don't know anymore. I don't need a man; I just think dying alone may be depressing.

My need to oppose the unfair Iranian girl conundrum is why I'm currently sitting in the passenger seat of Maziar's BMW as he drives us over to the coffee shop where we will meet my new realtor. Or, at least, potential new realtor. He still has to pass the good old-fashioned father-brother test.

I stare out the window, watching the trees breeze by as the leaves blur into a wave of green. I try to block out the chatter between Dad and Maziar. They talk too much, and I have a headache.

My mind wanders to the dinner that set the wheels in motion on my newest endeavor: buying a house. Despite the need for freedom, as it provides me a way to shake the chains my family has bound me with but are too oblivious to see, there's a part of me that's terrified of the magnitude of this commitment.

"I can't wait until you're sitting here with your husband too, Bita, and my grandchildren are surrounding me," Mom said dreamily. "Wouldn't that be nice?" She turned her lovesick gaze toward me then, and all I wanted to do was roll my eyes.

As if that weren't bad enough, Maziar thought he'd be the "good" brother that he thinks he is and jump in for the rescue. I didn't need saving, but no one seemed to realize that.

"Oh, leave her alone, Mom. She has plenty of time to get married," he replied, smiling at me. "Not all of us can be as lucky as me." Could he have been any more annoying? "Plus, no one is thinking babies yet. Just practicing." He winked at Sara, who turned the color of a cherry.

"Seriously, you guys are bordering intolerable right now." I finally allowed myself the eyeroll I'd been suppressing. "There's more to life than just getting married."

"Of course there is," Mom agreed. "But you've finished school and passed your exams. Now you're officially a dentist and we couldn't be prouder. What else is there for you to accomplish, though? You're getting older, *azizam.*" *My dearest.*

Now, just a few minutes out from our destination, I wish I hadn't let her get to me.

But the cultural expectations placed on young Iranian women are damn near impossible, really. We're encouraged to "stand on our own two feet," studying for careers that can support us without the help of a partner. But at the same time, we're urged to be on the prowl for a suitable husband. Suitable means hot, established, goal-driven, and loving. Like that's easy. When was I supposed to be on this husband hunt anyway? I spent half my life studying my ass off. In a library. Alone.

"You're right, Mom. I'm getting older and it's time I take the next step." Her eyes had lit up momentarily as I'd hoped they would. Then, I delivered the blow. I'm such a bitch. "I'm going to buy my own place."

I cringe in the passenger seat as I recall my impulsive, and very emotionally charged, reaction. Dad being the openminded, rational man he is, seemed to think this was a good idea. After giving me his lecture on all the expenses owning a house would require, and all the responsibilities I'd have, he gave in, taking Mom with him.

I hope I can make this work. Not so much because I'm afraid of failing, but more because coming back home after failing would give my brother enough ammunition to make me feel stupid until I'm on my deathbed, and Mom exactly what she needs to control me forever. Not making it at this one thing will tighten my chains to the point of suffocation.

I'm jarred from my thoughts when Maziar squeezes my wrist. I look around, realizing he's parked. It's go time.

"You ready?" The worry nestled in my brother's eyes makes the knot in my stomach multiply in size.

"Yup. I'm good," I lie. I slap on a winning smile and follow my family through the parking lot. I refuse to let my anxiety ruin this for me. I'm a grown-ass woman; I can do this.

"He comes highly recommended," Dad says, as we make our way toward the entrance to the coffee shop. "Shahram just used him to buy Banoo's first condo and they loved him."

"Okay, Dad. Whatever you think is best. We just need to get the process stared. It takes a while to find something," I reply.

"I don't know about using an Iranian realtor," Maziar teases. "I mean, you know how Iranians can be. He may screw us." He winks at me.

"Oh, Maziar, don't be so negative." Dad rolls his eyes. "And don't generalize people like that. We should support our community when we can. Let's talk to the poor guy before we decide on his intentions. That's the whole point of this meeting, anyway."

My brother loves messing with Dad, pushing his buttons when he can. A playful camaraderie is ever-present between the two of them. Sometimes, I feel like I've been left out of an inside joke that only they understand. Makes me wish I were a boy. Iranian men and their sons. Legacies to their names and reminders of who they used to be. Despite my being Daddy's girl, there's a bond there I can't compete with.

I head toward the coffee shop doors with Maziar and Dad flanking me, two soldiers in an unnecessary battle. This business of buying a house has proven tedious—first, with their lack of confidence in me, and now, stuck between the walls of their opinions. It's been a tennis match of locations, style, and budget. I just want my own place. I've grown weary of Mom's constant intrusion and Dad's never-ending guidance. I love my parents, but I'd prefer to love them from a distance.

The cold air rushes into our faces as Dad pulls open the door. It's a nice distraction from the heat bearing down on us as it bounces off the parking lot asphalt. The California summer sun is vicious, with little regard for sunburns and skin cancer.

A gentleman, possibly in his late thirties, looks up at us as we walk through the door. Recognition crosses his face and he stands, reaching out toward Dad when we approach his table.

"*Aghah* Parviz?" His brows rise in question. His perfectly etched arches catch my attention. Full yet tamed. The new fad among trendy Iranian men. They give women a run for their money when it comes to getting their eyebrows primped.

"*Salom* Ramtin, *khan*," Dad greets him.

The edges of his lips curl up further as he reaches over to take my hand. "Bita *khanoom*, I presume?"

Despite the tiny flutter beneath my ribcage, his attention doesn't linger on me too long, turning it back toward the men accompanying me. I can only guess he presumes the deciding factor of whether he gets signed on as my realtor lies with them. A single Iranian woman, regardless of her age, is always viewed as some sort of damsel in distress when her father or brother are around. Stereotypical for sure, but something in the way he flashes me a tiny grin before turning toward the men, softens the blow. Almost like he's humoring them and it's our little secret. It pulls at me, unexpectedly.

"Can I get you some coffee?" Ramtin asks, looking around the table.

Dad stands. "I'll get it," he says.

"No, Parviz *aghah*. *Khayesh meekonam. It's my pleasure.* I have this."

Taarof, the art of hospitality in the Iranian culture. It would be considered rude if Dad didn't offer to pay for his own family's drinks, as well as if Ramtin doesn't take the initiative to pay for it himself. Complicated and drawn out at times, but a popular Iranian social norm.

"*Merci*, Ramtin. I would love a cappuccino," Dad says, taking his seat.

Ramtin turns toward my brother and me. "And for you?"

"Thanks. I'll have one too," Maziar adds. "And Bita will have a regular coffee."

As Ramtin walks up to the counter, I elbow my brother in the side.

"What?" Maziar asks, innocently.

"I can speak for myself." I scowl at him. "You seem to forget who's the older sibling around here."

"Dude, relax. I just know you like regular coffee. I'm not taking away your womanhood or anything." He chuckles, arms raised in surrender.

"You're so damn annoying."

"Okay, okay. I won't order coffee for you anymore. Jeez, I was trying to be nice."

I glare at him. But when my brother leans in and pecks me on the cheek, I can't help but giggle. I'm such a sucker when it comes to him. Definitely a downfall.

Ramtin returns with our drinks and takes his seat. He immediately launches into questions, focused on his mission to get our business. We discuss desirable locations, town houses versus traditional homes, number of beds and baths. He's very smooth, the perfect combination of business class and downhome roots.

I lean back in my chair, the conversation barreling forward. Each question I answer is accompanied by both Maziar and Dad throwing in their opinions as well, giving me a moment to stare at Ramtin.

He's much older than me, but there's a childlike quality to him. Something in the deep set of his rich brown eyes feels adventurous. When he smiles, his plump lips stretch across his perfect teeth, exuding a charm that takes my breath away. I wouldn't say he's gorgeous, but nonetheless, there's something about him that makes me curious and has me intrigued.

"So, we want to mainly focus on single family dwellings, and possibly town houses?" he asks.

"Yeah, that sounds good," I answer.

"Do you really want a town house?" Maziar interjects. "You share a wall, and it could get loud if your neighbor isn't considerate." He turns toward Ramtin and starts listing pros and cons.

My attention is drawn to a tiny scar below Ramtin's left eye. It's small and oval, possibly from a bad bout of chicken pox. A tiny imperfection that somehow adds to his sex appeal.

"Does Saturday work for you?" he suddenly says.

"Huh, what?" I realize he's directing the question at me. I feel my cheeks burn and pray I don't appear red and blotchy.

Maziar and Dad just wait for me to respond, neither privy to the fact that I've been checking this guy out for the past hour. He isn't really my type, older than the men I usually date, so it would make sense they'd be oblivious.

"Saturday," I mumble.

"Yes, does that work for you to go look at some houses?" Ramtin repeats. He chuckles, and there's that twinkle again. It makes my skin prickle.

"Uhm, yeah. That should be fine."

He watches me for a moment longer than he should, making my stomach knot, then he looks away as he gathers his papers.

"Then I'll see you all this weekend."

He stands and I take in his long, lean form. The cobra shape of his torso and the way his shirt is pulled tight over his biceps puts my generation to shame. He's not buff by industry standards, just sharply defined.

How old is he? Sadly, the conversation never progresses to more personal terrain, and I leave the coffee shop under a barrage of commentary from Dad and Maziar, ruining my daydream buzz.

* * *

"The bedroom is kind of small." I make a slow lap within its four walls.

"Okay, that's good to know," Ramtin says.

He's leaning against the door frame, arms across his chest. His six-foot build, slim and runner-like, only takes up half the space. The light from the window down the hall outlines his body in a luminescent glow, accentuating the rise and fall of his chest beneath his shirt.

The crisp white button up he wears amplifies his olive-toned skin, complemented further by the opposing dark shade of his jeans. His lids are framed by long lashes and his eyebrows are in pristine condition, as usual. A grin subtly plays at the corner of his full lips.

For a moment I'm transported into an alternate universe, one I've been popping in and out of in my head the past few weeks while house hunting, where Ramtin is mine and we're out browsing locations for our first home together. I imagine he'd rest against the wall like so, waiting for me to fully absorb the feel of our potential dwelling place.

He's old enough to be my dad. Okay, maybe not that old, but still. I was able to discover he's forty-three, so I guess he could technically have fathered me, if he knocked someone up at fourteen.

Mom and Dad make it down the hallway, their conversation pulling me out of my daydream. *Why am I even thinking about this guy that way? Is he my type?*

I really don't know what my type is. With very little experience in the arena of relationships, I still haven't figured it out. I usually go for the typical Iranian guys, the ones my friends drool over because they're hot, driven, and my age. But they're always too cocky and full of themselves to think about being anything other than the goodtime guy. Those guys don't work out well for me. Their immaturity causes me to lose interest quickly. *Why haven't I ever dated an older man?*

I turn to face the window, busying myself by taking in the view of the neighborhood. Honestly, I'm just no longer able to stare at Ramtin as he watches me with little interest further than the current possibility of a sale. I'm over here planning out futures that don't seem to be near his radar.

Three houses in, I realize I needed to downsize my idea of what I could afford. Dad's helping me with the down payment, but I'm determined to do this "adulting" business on my own. I need to stand on my own two feet, show myself that I can really do this grownup thing. We can't all be Peter Pan.

"It's cute, isn't it, Bita?" Mom asks, as Ramtin steps aside to let her pass. "The bedrooms are slightly small, but it's quaint and in such a fabulous neighborhood. It'll be easy to rent once you get married."

I have to consciously keep myself from flinching. She discusses my future as if marriage is the only outcome. What if I never find a guy I love enough to marry? Because, let's be honest here, being single indefinitely is a real possibility. But I don't say that to Mom. It would only spark a debate I really don't feel like engaging in. Plus, for some odd reason I don't yet understand, the idea of discussing my inability to find a mate while Ramtin is in earshot is humiliating.

"I agree with your mom. This is good for you, *dokhtaram*. You don't need too much space right now when it's just you," Dad joins in.

And there it is, reference two, albeit subtly, to the lack of a husband.

"Well, I personally love this neighborhood and think it's a great little place where Bita could set down her own roots," Ramtin suddenly says.

My parents fall silent, exchanging wide-eyed expressions. I spare a quick glance in Ramtin's direction and he winks at me, flashing his perfect smile, making my stomach drop into my toes. *He doesn't think my only outcome to success is through a husband.* I try to hide the smirk curling the edges of my lips.

"We have a few more houses to look at before you need to make a decision, Bita," Ramtin adds. "If you're ready, we can head to the next one."

"Yeah, I'm ready." I follow Ramtin down the hall, wondering how this stranger somehow managed to leave my parents speechless. I'm not entirely sure, but the warmth growing in the pit of my stomach is a sure indication that he has my attention.

We make it to three more houses before we part ways.

"I really liked that first one," Mom decides, as we drive home.

"Yes, it was the best location. Your mom's right, it will be easy to rent with its proximity to the beach."

I'm glad my parents have their priorities straight. Always hovering in the back of each conversation: when will she get married? Add a younger brother that just tied the knot, and the pressure is on.

I turn and lean my head against the backseat window, feeling the warmth from the sun. I stare out onto the streets of Santa Monica, watching couples walking hand in hand along the sidewalk. A sigh escapes me, a longing I try to deny, pushing to the surface. Despite my protests, I do dream of finding "the one." Maybe that makes me weak, or maybe it's just human nature. But a life of solitude scares me a little.

As we stop at a red light, a couple embraces. He leans down and kisses the crown of her head, and I'm oddly reminded of Ramtin. What would it feel like to have his strong arms wrapped around my waist, and the afternoon stubble on his face playfully scratch my skin as he kisses me?

We drive on, and as the image of the couple embracing shrinks in my line of vision, so do the possibilities I've let run rampant in my mind all afternoon. Daydreams of Ramtin evaporate with the summer heat, taking with them the little bubbles of hope that had begun to form.

CHAPTER TWO

I t took me an hour to get ready to go work out. Ridiculous, I
know. Now I'm clad in my Lululemon black cropped leggings,
and a hot pink sports bra, peeking out from beneath my black
tank. My hair is pulled up in a messy bun, which realistically took me
twenty minutes to create, for the perfect combination of "I threw it up
in a hurry" and "my hair is just that awesome." I have only a little
makeup on, enough to create a smooth finish to my skin, and some
eyeliner, accentuating the green in my eyes.

My sister-in-law likes to tell me they remind her of the snake from
the Jungle Book story. I'm pretty sure his eyes are bright yellow, and
equally sure, it used to be an insult she now uses to tease me with. It's
cool. She's allowed a few freebies as payback for the royal bitch I was
when she met my brother. However, now, every time I line them, I
can't help but hear that damn snake's voice hissing in my ears.

I push through the doors of the gym and try to discreetly search
the premises. Ramtin told me he'd leave my name at the front desk
with my day pass. I'm not sure if that means he's currently here
working out, or if he's even planning on meeting me, but I do know
that my stomach is uneasy with the anticipation of possibly
seeing him.

Initially, he's nowhere to be found. I try to stay calm, reminding myself there's an entire gym left to walk through. The young lady at the desk asks for my ID and then has me fill out a waiver. She's about to take me on the grand tour, when I hear his voice.

"Leslie, I can show her around, if that's cool?"

Ramtin is standing a short distance behind me, the heat from his body closing the distance between us. I inhale, taking in the mingling smell of shampoo and cleanliness he wears. My eyelids flutter shut as euphoria takes over. How does this man have such a strange effect on me? Or maybe it's not strange but rather what attraction and interest is supposed to feel like? All I know is that if I had ever felt like this before, marriage wouldn't feel like such a distant possibility.

"Sure," Leslie says, blushing beneath his gaze.

Watching her cheeks flush makes me feel less idiotic. The comfortable tone in her voice makes me jealous.

"Great!" He steps up beside me. "Ready for your tour?" There's an enthusiasm in his tone, but to my dismay, nothing else. I know what it looks like when a man flirts with a woman, and this isn't it.

"Yeah, I'm ready."

He walks me through the various levels of the gym. The muscle head in the weight room, the lean runner pounding the treadmill at full speed, and the tall, dark, and handsome gentleman who bumps into us as we pass by the locker rooms, double-take when I walk by. Their pheromones slam into me, present and undeniable. But my companion is neither moved nor interested. He doesn't even notice, and if he does, it leaves him unaffected. Disappointment lies heavy in my chest, mingled with irritation.

"I'll be in the weight room," he says, dropping me off at the elliptical machines.

I don't know why I thought we'd work out together, but a blaze of anger sets me on fire. How dare he brush me off so nonchalantly! He should feel lucky that my twenty-eight-year-old self wants to hang out with him. Any other fortysomething would be all over me, lapping up any attention I give him, like a loyal puppy. *The nerve of this guy!*

"Cool." I step onto the machine, busying myself with the dials.

I don't spare him another glance, not one that he could notice. I follow his departure in the reflection of the window, forcing myself not to turn around. He makes his way to the other room, disappearing beneath the halogen lights.

I shake off the blow of defeat and crank up the resistance on the machine. It's so high I'm sweating within the first two minutes. Once I'm done, I hop onto the treadmill, getting lost in the sound of my feet slapping against the belt, in rhythm to the music blasting in my headphones.

By the time I make it over to the weight room, I'm drenched, and I don't give a shit. It's not like Ramtin gives a crap about how I look anyway. I find him in the far corner facing the wall-length mirror. He has earbuds on and sweat dampens his forehead each time he pulls the bar up to his chest. There are three large plates attached to each end. I have no idea how heavy the weights are, but judging from his concentration, it's a struggle.

Each muscle is strained beneath his t-shirt. Veins bulge along his arms, small road maps my fingers itch to trace. His skin glistens with perspiration, and I want nothing more than to pull the shirt up over his head so I can get a better look at the hills and valleys that lay beneath. But instead, I strut toward the opposite end of the mirror, feigning indifference, and pick up two dumbbells, busying myself with bicep curls.

One of the young bodybuilder types standing beside me strikes up a conversation. I humor him, acting as though he has clever things to say. I giggle, staring up at him while I bat my lashes. I reach out and gently place my hand on his large arm, drawing my finger across his skin, focused as he speaks.

In the reflection of the mirror, my eyes lock on Ramtin's. He's watching me, expressionless. For a moment, I think I see something flash across his face. Anger? Irritation? Hopefully jealousy. But as quickly as it comes, it disappears, lost in the clinging and clanking of the weights around us. Annoyed, I break off the conversation with Mr. Bodybuilder and excuse myself.

"I'm finished," I announce abruptly as I approach Ramtin.

He lets the weight he's holding drop to the floor with a thud.

"Cool," he answers. "What did you think?" His expression is

unreadable, the lines of concentration smoothed out across his forehead, now. When he smiles, I want to reach out and slap him in frustration. What do I need to do to get this guy's attention? Prance around naked? Even then, I'm not sure he'd spare me a second glance.

"It's a nice gym. Thanks for getting me a pass."

"No problem. Maybe I'll see you around."

"Yeah."

When he lightly squeezes my arm, I want to stomp my feet and storm out of the gym, which only makes me feel like more of a child. My ego has taken a beating and I hate that I can't turn his head.

"Bye."

I spin on my heels and quickly make my way to the parking lot, convincing myself that distance is the best remedy. The farther away from Ramtin I get, the easier it will become to forget how little I was able to pique his interest. I know I can't expect to be everyone's cup of tea, but shit, this just makes me feel like crap about myself.

CHAPTER THREE

I'm walking past a furniture store just as two girls come tumbling out, the older one playfully pinching her sister as the younger one laughs while brushing her hand away. I stop, giving them a wide berth to complete their sisterly game.

The tall, lean one appears ballerina-esque as she sashays behind her sister. Her grin is mischievous and protective. There's a familiarity about her that I can't place. I'm not sure where I'd know a teenager from.

"Oh, sorry," she apologizes, when she realizes I'm waiting for them to finish.

"No worries," I reply. They move over on the sidewalk giving me room to pass. I take a few steps and am stopped short when I hear my name.

"Bita?" His voice is smooth and thick. I don't even need to turn around to know who he is. My stomach instinctively quivers.

"Hey," I say, turning to face Ramtin.

"How are you?"

"Good, thanks. And you?" I ask.

"I'm well. I haven't seen you at the gym lately."

He's intently focused on me and his eldest doesn't seem to

appreciate it. Out of the corner of my eye, I can see a scowl forming on her face. Her head's bobbing between her father and me, each additional word only adding to the ever-growing pink creeping up her neck. The younger sibling is smiling at us, oblivious.

"I've been going early in the morning. Before work. I'm so tired afterwards that I get too lazy. Rather get it out of the way first thing." I don't want to tell him I'm dragging myself out of bed at some ungodly hour trying to avoid running into him.

Between Ramtin's fierce gaze and his daughter's imaginary daggers, I'm lightheaded.

"Oh, okay. Glad you ended up getting a membership. Maybe I'll meet you one of these mornings." He grins, an uncharacteristic interest in his eyes.

Is he flirting with me? I can't help but smile back. This is the first time he's ever been somewhat uninhibited. I'm digging it, until his daughter steps in and ruins my mood.

"Dad, is Mom coming? I thought we were all going to lunch." She emphasizes *all* as she glares in my direction.

"Oh, Bita, this is my daughter, Yasi. And that's Kimiya." He points over to the younger girl. Yasi's disdain is permanently fixed on her face, but Kimiya just waves, a sweet kindness stretching across hers. Despite not looking like her father, she reminds me of him in the energy she has about her.

"Hi."

As if on cue, a tall blonde goddess walks out of the furniture store. She's only a few inches shorter than her ex-husband, her body stretched and flawless. I imagine daily bouts of yoga and the gym have molded her muscles into the perfection standing before me. She glides, rather than walks, toward her daughters.

Her sleek straight hair reaches to the small of her back, thick bleached strands brushing her bare shoulders on the way down. I instinctively twist a strand of my own jet-black hair around my finger as it pales in comparison.

Her gaze sweeps across my frame, taking in my appearance. I have to force myself not to fidget, swallowing past my now parched throat.

"Who's this, Ramtin?" There's a hint of an Iranian accent on the edge of her words, so subtle you'd miss it, if you weren't Persian yourself.

"Roya, this is Bita. Bita this is Roya," Ramtin introduces. "I helped Bita buy her house recently."

"Nice to meet you," I say.

She smiles. "Likewise." Then turns her attention onto her girls, no longer bothered to acknowledge my presence. "You guys ready to eat?" she asks them.

"Yes! I'm starving," Yasi confirms. She throws her arms up dramatically. Definitely Oscar-worthy. "Can we go already?" Her voice drops into a childish whine. They should really think about putting this girl in acting.

"Of course, *joonam, my soul,*" Roya answers. "Let's go, Ramtin. The girls are hungry." She glances over her shoulder at me. "Nice meeting you, Bita." At least she attempts to hide her disgust behind a mediocre grin, unlike her daughter, who's still mentally shooting blades into my body.

Ramtin looks at me apologetically. "See you around, Bita." He turns and heads down the block with his family.

I stare at their backs as they walk away, realizing that the daydreams I've been harboring about Ramtin are just that. Hopeful, fun, make-believe that I like to get lost in. But it's clear reality is more complicated than I'd imagined. The obstacles between us are much larger than my insecurities. There's time, babies, and a past I can't compete with. And I'm not entirely sure I want to.

* * *

"He's cute," Shiva points out. She's looking at the gentleman Parisa just left behind at the other table.

"Please, he isn't doing anything with his life. So, who cares," Parisa replies.

"He's trying to get into law school," Maral says in his defense.

"Yeah, but we're almost thirty. I don't have time to wait for someone to go to law school. He should have done that a long time ago." Parisa brushes off Maral's comment like it's ludicrous. "Now that guy, his family is rich. And he just finished medical school."

"How does that make him any different? He doesn't have his life together yet either," I protest.

"Uhm, did you not hear me? His family is loaded." She winks at us and makes her way over to Hooman, her sights set on a target.

Have my friends always been this way? Or did they warp into bitches with age? I remember when we were in high school, lying on my bed, flipping through magazines as we built fantasy lives for ourselves in our heads. We didn't know who we'd marry, but we just wanted to fall in love. We never discussed bank accounts and brand names in our daydreams. When did it all get so shallow?

I scan the private room at Cleo's, no longer in the mood to contemplate my current friendships. They'd require I look at myself as well. Maybe I'm as vain as they are, and I've just never realized it.

I pull my attention to the splashes of teal green worked throughout the room, instead. They complement the warm brown tones of the walls. A color scheme to consider if I redo my new place.

There are circular designs painted along the edges of the ceiling. Bands of what look like Arabic letters woven together in a soft tribal design. I have no idea if they really are part of the alphabet, or just shaped that way. Since I'm Jewish, Hebrew is more my forte. But regardless, it's a beautifully subtle way of working the culture into the décor. Tasteful and eye-catching.

Parvin waltzes over to us and clinks her wine glass against our drinks.

"Thanks for making it out, ladies!" she squeals. Her voice is high-pitched and now slurred, from the multiple alcoholic beverages guests have bought for the birthday girl. She throws her arm around my neck. "Why don't we hang out more, Bita? We should really hang out." She kisses my cheek hard, then giggles as she sways on her feet.

I look at Maral and Shiva and roll my eyes, laughing. Drunk girls are entertaining.

I'm not really in the mood to party tonight. I volunteered as designated driver, so I sip on my tonic water and people watch. I know most of the guests; we all grew up in the same circles and frequent the same parties. Close-knit Iranian communities. Everyone knows everyone. And also, everyone's business. It's somewhat suffocating.

I've been feeling out of sorts the past few days and I can't shake it. I love the fact that I'm out on my own. Having my personal space is divine. However, there are moments I can't help but feel lonely. I'm a creature that craves human connection. I like the bustle of family and friends around me all the time.

Our house was always full. Maziar and I had friends over every day, and on the weekends, my parents had *mehmoonies, gatherings,* with their friends. Very rarely was our home calm and quiet; always someone to hang out with. Sometimes, the silence in my house presses down on me with the weight of my solitude.

Running into Ramtin yesterday, didn't help either. A reminder of how desperate I've become that I'm pining over an older man. Who couldn't give two shits about me, for that matter.

"Hi, Bita." A voice pulls me out of my thoughts.

"Oh, hey, Pouyah. How are you?"

"I'm good. It's been a long time," he says. "How are you? How's your family? I heard your brother got married."

"Yeah, he did."

His tongue runs across his lips, pulling the lower one between his teeth. A habit he's had since we were ten. One I've never really noticed until this moment.

Did he suddenly get hot? Or am I just lonely and horny? Truthfully, who cares? Judging from the way he's looking at me, I've spontaneously become beautiful, too.

"Can I get you a drink?"

"No, thanks," I answer. "Designated driver."

"Well, what are you drinking?" he asks, pointing to the glass nestled between my fingers.

"Just tonic water."

"Then tonic water it is." He winks, as he reaches out to take my now empty cup.

His wavy dark hair is slicked back, and his oddly gray eyes are stark against his tan background. He heads back toward the bar, located outside in the main hall. It gives me time to drool over him without him seeing.

He's not as tall as I'd like; he only has a few inches on me with my heels. But his frame is wide and tank-like. His obsession with CrossFit has clearly paid off. His button-up is barely hanging on, stretched to the max, ready to burst at the seams. I'm not into the buff types, but damn, he looks good right now.

As he walks back toward me with the drinks, he smiles, two deep dimples making a glorious appearance. I'm imagining him naked before he's even made it to the table.

He hands me the tonic water and clinks his glass against mine.

"Cheers."

"Cheers." I giggle and flip my hair, peering up through hooded lids. I'm laying it on thick, but he doesn't seem to mind. I lean in closer. "I just got my own place," I whisper.

I'm not sure what I'm doing here, never the type for one-night stands, but something inside me has burst open and common sense has died along with it. I'm no longer burdened with what people may think if they find out that "Bita is gallivanting around town." Matter of fact, let them talk. The next big Iranian scandal. I don't want to be alone tonight.

"Really?" he asks. Mischief flashes in the tug of his lips.

"Yup," I reply. "You should come by and see it sometime."

"I'd love that."

Just as I am going to invite him over for the night, Shiva bursts through the crowd.

"Oh, there you are," she announces, flustered. Her eyelids are droopy, and her lisp is more noticeable than usual. "We have to go. Parisa's in the bathroom puking."

"What? When I left you guys, she was fine."

"Yeah, I know. But then she thought taking three tequila shots with Peyman and his friends was a good flirting tactic," she says. "She started out drinking vodka. She obviously didn't get the memo about mixing alcohol." Shiva rolls her eyes, then notices that Pouyah is standing beside her. "Hey, Pouyah. Sorry for breaking up the party." She waves her hand between the two of us indicating *we* are the party. *Were* the party, more like it. Until Parisa decided to cockblock, or whatever the female equivalent is. "Maral has her outside waiting at the valet."

"Shit, okay. Let's go." I turn toward Pouyah. "I'm sorry. Rain check?"

"Most definitely." He flashes those irresistible dimples again.

My heart flip-flops in my chest, followed by the crash of disappointment at the potential of what I'm missing tonight. And when he leans in to hug me, the scent of his cologne fills my body with a longing so intense I'm convinced I could murder Parisa and get rid of her body in the dumpster out back. But instead of the death penalty, I allow myself to linger in his embrace for a moment longer, before pulling away. He winks at me as Shiva grabs my hand and drags me toward the front door. Damn my friends for ruining this potential escapade for me.

I don't turn around to see if he's watching, but I can feel the weight of his gaze on me as I make it through the crowd. I sway my hips a little more profoundly and hope it makes him as annoyed about the lost opportunity as I am. Just as we turn to exit the restaurant, I glance back at Pouyah, confirming I still have his attention.

CHAPTER FOUR

There's a knock at the door. I look up at the clock on the microwave. Eight-thirty in the morning. I'm not expecting anyone.

I shuffle over to the front door, my fuzzy bedroom slippers swooshing across the hardwood floors. They're a perfect complement to my puppy-clad fleece pajama bottoms and my worn-out matching gray t-shirt. I push a strand of hair away from my face, it having escaped the messy bun sitting in the middle of my head.

I stand on my tiptoes to look through the peephole, and my heart stops. Ramtin is standing a few feet outside on the patio.

He's in a pair of black shorts and a blue tank top, his Nikes in perfect color coordination. The breath stops somewhere between my lungs and throat, my body paralyzed until he reaches out and rings the doorbell, jarring me into motion.

With shaky fingers, I undo the chain and deadbolt, slowly swinging the door open. I remember a moment too late that I look like a train wreck.

"Hey," he says. He's smiling broadly, harboring entirely too much energy this early on a Saturday morning.

"Hi." I search my mind trying to remember if I had some belated appointment with him in regards to the house. But I haven't spoken to him in weeks.

"I hope it's okay that I just stopped by. Maybe I should have called first." His lids scrunch with concern as he notices my outfit.

"No, it's fine. Come in," I answer, remembering my manners. I step aside, giving him passage, using the moment to try to smooth down my unruly hair. It's useless.

"I'm sorry. Were you still sleeping?"

Ugh! I look like crap! "No," I reply. This is so not how I envisioned our next encounter. I can't help laughing at my luck. "I just look this bad at eight on a Saturday morning."

The tension relaxes out of his posture. "You look amazing at eight on a Saturday morning."

His comment is so unexpected that I stop mid-giggle and just stare at him. He blatantly told me I was pretty, without a care to the possibility of my rejection. The confidence he exudes is so damn sexy, quite a contradiction to the younger, more fragile men of my generation. It draws me in even further. I don't even bother trying to hide my surprise, or the heat flushing my cheeks. I don't care if he can tell I'm swooning, because at this moment, I'm swooning.

"I was in the mood for a morning hike, and there's a really great trail a few blocks away from your house. I just thought I'd stop by and see if you were interested. It's always more fun with company."

He has a sheepish grin and his expression reminds me of a teenage boy asking a girl out to a dance. There's also that fire again, burning brightly in the back of his eyes. My heart quickens.

"You want me to go hiking with you?"

"Yes," he confirms. "If you want to."

Of course I want to. I want to do anything that puts you in my hemisphere. "Sure. I'd love to."

I stare up at him, mesmerized as usual. I can't help but be giddy at the fact that Ramtin came to my house with the excuse of hiking. Most days, I'd take it at face value, but judging from the way he's looking at me, I'm going to say there may be something more to this morning. Or at least, I'm hoping there is.

"Want some coffee?" I ask. "I have a fresh pot in the kitchen. Help yourself while I change." With that, I turn and head toward my bedroom.

I shut the door softly, then proceed to run around my room like a Tasmanian devil as I fling clothes onto my closet floor trying to figure out what to wear. I can't get too dolled up, as he's already seen me in all my Saturday morning glory, and I don't want to appear like I'm trying too hard. Instead, I mimic his own outfit, donning on my own pair of shorts and tank. I choose gray paired with a green shirt, hoping it emphasizes my eyes. I leave my hair up in a messy-ish bun but pull the unwanted loose strands back into it, strategically leaving a few face framing pieces. One dab of lip gloss later, I head back into the living room.

Ramtin is standing with his back halfway turned, so I have a view of his profile. He's staring at my neighbor's toddler playing with his trucks on their lawn. He's holding a cup of coffee a few inches from his lips, the steam immersing his expression in a dream like haze. Amusement lingers on his lips as his gaze tracks the path of the Tonka trucks. The toddler crashes them together and makes explosive gestures with his hands. I step up beside him and we both watch the baby play, in silence.

"Children are amazing," he finally says. "They have yet to be jaded by the world, so their creativity and hopefulness pours out of them in abundance. I always feel like a better version of myself around my kids."

I don't have much to add to the sentiment, since I don't have any children of my own. I know that the idea is to get married and have babies, but I've been focused on the married part and forgotten about the baby portion.

"I guess I'd like kids someday. I haven't really thought about it."

He doesn't look at me, just continues to stare at the little boy across the street. His lids tighten creating a web of lines that fan out across his skin, as his brows pinch together in thought. When he lifts the mug to his lips and takes a sip, the steam submerges his features into an omniscient haze.

"You should," he replies. "You're young, and there's plenty of time for that still."

His voice is even and calm, but his body betrays him, the muscles in his shoulders and back tensed and coiled. An odd reaction, because I don't understand why my desire to have children, or not, would have that effect on him. He shakes it off quickly, though, a sweet smile nestling on his face before he turns toward me. But I can see that he doesn't feel it.

"You ready to go?" he asks.

"Yeah." *Did I say something wrong? Should I not have said anything about kids?* I'm not sure, but he doesn't leave me time to figure it out, launching into motion.

"Okay, let's go!" He's entirely too energetic. It comes out forced and fake, only adding to the knots forming in the pit of my stomach. "We don't want to hit the heat. And it's a decent trail, so it will take us a little bit of time."

He pulls his keys out of his pocket and heads toward the front door. I follow obediently, still trying to figure out what the hell just happened to change the mood between us. He's a few paces ahead of me as if he's trying to keep his distance, which only confuses me further. The hope I felt when I saw him standing at my door, crumbles around me and dissipates into the breeze. *Did I interpret it all wrong? Maybe he just doesn't have any friends?*

He opens the door for me but stands back far enough that I can't possibly brush up against him when I take my seat. I feel like a child who's just been designated with cooties. Irritation burns through me. I hold onto it, because if I don't, I may lose it. This emotional roller coaster I've found myself on is giving me a headache. I want off.

"Did I say something wrong?" I blurt out as soon as he gets in the car. I'm not going to play games. This isn't good for my sanity, and besides, he's annoying the hell out of me right now.

"What?" The confusion in his piercing eyes only fuels my fire further.

"Did I say something to offend you?" I ask again. "We seemed okay, and then you asked me about kids and the next thing I know, you're suddenly clamming up. I'm just trying to figure out what I said to change your mood."

He blinks a few times, his arm suspended midair, on the way to the ignition. I think I may be more straightforward than he was expecting. I have to suppress a laugh. This entire thing is crazy. One step forward and ten steps back. I have no idea what we're doing here.

His expression softens. "No, you didn't say anything wrong. I'm sorry," he adds, reaching across the center console and squeezing my hand. The feel of his palm, rough and rugged on my skin, soothes the burning inside me. He allows his fingers to linger and I have to fight the urge to intertwine mine with his. Just like that, I'm back to a puddle on the floor.

"Then why the sudden attitude change?" I ask.

"No attitude change. I just forget how young you are sometimes. That's all."

"I'm not that young," I protest. I have to consciously keep the whine out of my tone. No use sounding like a child. It won't help my case.

"Well, you're much younger than I am, anyway."

* * *

Two Saturdays later, I'm clad in workout clothes and a tight braid, a half-hour before Ramtin's due to arrive. I sit at my kitchen table, thumbing through my emails, waiting. Suddenly, a black Mercedes pulls into my driveway.

Shit! What is Sara doing here?

I stare as my sister-in-law gets out of her car and heads to the front door with Starbucks in hand. She doesn't notice me watching her as she clumsily balances one cup on top of the other, trying to ring the doorbell. Even though I know she's standing there, the sound of bells chiming still surprises me.

I quickly check the clock on my wall. Ramtin will be here in twenty minutes. That's not enough time to get rid of her! Panic settles into my limbs, making my fingers go numb.

No one knows Ramtin and I are spending time together, not even Shiva. There hasn't been any reason to share it with anyone. It's new, and nothing has happened. I don't even understand what's going on between us, if anything at all.

But I really don't want her to find out and tell Maziar. They tell each other everything. It's sickening, really. All I need is for my brother to launch in on an inquisition and possibly try to ruin everything if he doesn't agree. *This could be bad.*

"Hey!" I chirp, when I open the door. "I wasn't expecting you." My smile is tight and possibly unnatural. I'm hoping Sara doesn't notice. Along with the sheen of sweat currently forming across my forehead.

"Hi!" When I don't say anything, she thrusts the coffee in my direction. "I brought you a latte."

"Thanks." I take the cup from her outstretched hand.

"Can I come in?" she asks. Confusion pinches her brows at my lack of manners.

"Oh, shoot. Yes, of course. Sorry. I don't know what's wrong with me. I'm tired," I explain, with a nervous giggle. "I'm a bit slow."

Her expression softens. "No worries. It's early. I wasn't even sure you'd be awake." She takes in my outfit as she steps past me into the living room. "Are you going to the gym?"

"Um," I stutter. "No, I'm planning on going for a hike with a friend."

She stares at me, her gaze boring holes into my defenses. I'm convinced she's rummaging through my brain as we speak.

"Friend." She draws out the word as she smirks. "Which friend?"

Shit. Shit. Shit.

I don't know what to say, but it seems fate isn't going to give me the option to decide. As if on cue, Ramtin steps up to the front door, which I'm still holding open. I can tell he's here from the way Sara steps to her left to get a better look. If she's confused at who the older gentleman at my door is, she doesn't let on.

"Hi," Ramtin says. His voice is thick and gritty with the early morning.

"Hi," Sara replies, stepping around me. Her hand is outstretched and as Ramtin takes it, she adds, "I'm Sara. Bita's sister-in-law." She waits expectantly for Ramtin to introduce himself since my tongue has taken a leave absence.

"Nice to meet you, Sara. I'm Ramtin."

Recognition crosses Sara's face as she connects the dots. It's evident in the shocked expression she quickly throws in my direction that's she's figured it out.

"You too," she answers.

He looks between the two of us, and then at the Starbucks cups in our hands.

"Did I interrupt something? Did you tell me you couldn't go hiking today and I just got it mixed up, Bita?"

The sound of my name leaving his lips causes chills to run up my spine.

"No, I was just in the neighborhood and stopped by to drop something off for Bita. As well as bring her some coffee." She lifts her cup as proof. "I was just leaving." Sara doesn't miss a beat, her ruse natural and believable. "I'll see you later?" She waits patiently for me to silently confirm I'll be letting her in on my little secret.

"Yeah. Sure," I reply. I must look like a moron, wide-eyed and nervous at a simple encounter. But it isn't that simple, is it? Now I have to explain to Sara. Which I don't want to do.

"Have fun hiking," she adds. Her voice is bubbly and lighthearted, a complete contradiction to the way I feel in this moment. "Call me later?"

"Yup, I sure will."

Then she prances off to her car. Ramtin and I watch as she pulls out of the driveway.

"She seems nice," he remarks.

"Yeah, she is."

"Are you ready?" he asks, turning toward me.

"Yes." I grab my keys and step onto the porch to meet him, locking the door behind me.

Once inside the car, he suddenly leans over and gently pushes a strand of hair behind my ear. His fingertips run softly along my cheek bone, whispering across my skin. Goosebumps invade my flesh and my blood warms as it rushes through my veins. I can hear it thrumming in my ears. I get the urge to lean across the center console and press my lips against his, the perfect first-kiss moment.

Before I have a chance to act impulsively, he realizes what he's doing and immediately severs the connection between us. He gathers himself up and quickly redirect his attention to the hike at hand.

"Let's go," he says, turning his car on.

Just like that, it's back to business, and I wonder if I dreamt it all up. But there's no denying the hope I can distinctly feel taking shape in my stomach, despite Ramtin's inconsistent behavior.

"Okay," I reply, smiling.

He winks at me, before putting the car in drive. *Score!*

* * *

We head up the dusty trail, the blazing sun bouncing its heat off each grain of sand, burning my skin. If not for the sunscreen he forced me to slather all over, I'd already be red and itchy. I'm happy I didn't resist, despite how annoyed I was at the fatherly gesture.

It's a quiet morning, only the birds and animals around to keep us company. I welcome the vacancy and silence as we head up the trail. There are eucalyptus and oak trees flanking either side, providing sporadic areas of cover as we make our way up the mountain to Inspiration Point. *I have a few things I'm hoping it inspires.*

In the spring, the shrubbery is green and lush. But in the summer heat, it's dead, leaving a landscape of browns and wilted tans, a corpse of its normal beauty. I don't mind. The view I'm staring at has me focused on things like tight biceps and defined calves. I'm too busy memorizing each curve and bulge to worry about anything else.

"Did you always want to be a dentist?" Ramtin asks, out of the blue.

"Um, not exactly," I answer, trying to focus on the conversation and not Ramtin's physique. "I was just always good at the sciences, so something in the medical field seemed like the rational way to go."

"That makes sense. But how did you pick dentistry? Did you flip a coin?" he jokes. His smile can make the deepest parts of me tremble.

"Would you think bad of me if I said yes?" I raise my brow and smirk.

"Nothing could make me think bad of you." It comes out low and quiet, almost a whisper.

The tenderness in his voice, the thoughtful pull in his eyes, stop me from breathing. But as soon as it comes, it's gone like the wind. The tiny glimpses into something deeper than just friendship have me dazed. I never know which Ramtin to expect, the older, fatherly friend, or the one who just might be thinking of me in ways that I'm thinking of him. I prefer the latter, and I'm always hit with a wave of sadness when he disappears, shoving his emotions back into the box and locking them up.

"So how did you choose?"

"Well, I just weighed the pros and cons, really. There was the idea of being an MD, but then there was entirely too much schooling involved. I really didn't want to devote another eight years of my life to studying. That left optometry and dentistry. The two *other* acceptable careers for Persians."

He laughs. "I love that. This whole notion that Iranian kids must either be doctors or lawyers. Apparently the only two respectable outcomes."

"It's stupid," I say, realizing he's neither. I'm hoping I haven't offended him, but his casual demeanor eases my anxious energy. "Honestly, dentistry just sounded better than optometry to me, that's all," I shrug. "Plus, I love my dentist. He's friends with my dad, so he's like family. Sounded like a good choice."

"I don't know how I feel about that. My dentist choosing her career on a whim," he kids.

"Well, good thing I'm not your dentist," I tease.

He laughs, bumps me with his hip, and winks.

"I'll race you up the hill," he taunts, then takes off at a slow jog.

I speed past him, yelling over my shoulder, giggling. "Please tell me you're holding back because you think I can't hang. Otherwise, this is just pathetic."

"*Ha!* I was just trying to be a gentleman," he replies as he makes his way to me. He pulls on my arm playfully, slowing me down as he pretends to try to get ahead. Then he grabs my hand and pulls me up the hill behind him.

The sensation of his fingers wrapped around mine feel like home. There's a connection and familiarity between us that makes no sense because I haven't known him long, nor do I know him well. But I do know I've never felt this before. With anyone.

I haven't met a man quite like Ramtin before. Maybe it's his age, but the fact that he seems to know exactly who he is turns me on. Guys in their twenties are still trying to figure it all out. Hell, I'm still trying to piece together who I am. But the way he's so comfortable in his skin draws me to him. All this time, I thought I was so focused on getting my own life together that I had no time to invest in relationships and setting roots with someone. But I'm slowly starting to realize that time was never the issue. I just hadn't met anyone who spoke to my soul.

Somewhere in a past life, Ramtin was mine and I was his. There's no other way to explain this instant connection I feel. And in this life, I'm sure that there's nothing more I want than to repeat history.

CHAPTER FIVE

I wait, impatiently staring out of the restaurant window. Ramtin is fifteen minutes late, and despite not wanting to panic, I am. It's been well over a month that we've engaged in biweekly morning hikes and coffee, his 50/50 custody obligations keeping him tied up otherwise.

The casual, friendly vibe hasn't evolved into much else. Every time it appears we may be making headway, he changes course. The flirtatious moments I think I see quickly disappear, causing me to wonder if I've imagined it all. It's an endless road of uncertainty.

However, this morning when he rushed off to a prior engagement, he suggested we take a rain check and meet up for dinner. I couldn't help but get excited. This could be the evening that changes it all, pushes us past the realm of "just friends." I'm hoping, anyway.

But now I sit at the table alone, dread swimming in my stomach as I continue to glance at my watch every thirty seconds, praying he isn't standing me up. Learning that I have indeed been imaging his advances would suck but being stood up in order to drive the point home would be horrifying.

My fingers balance above my home screen, debating whether I should send him a text asking if he's okay, when the hostess catches my eye. Standing behind her, appearing flustered, is Ramtin. My heart drops with relief. *Thank God.*

"I'm so sorry," he apologizes, immediately.

"It's okay."

"No, it isn't," he responds. "Being late is so rude, but I assure you I have a good reason."

I lean forward on the table, cocking my head to one side, and smirk.

"Okay, I'm listening," I say, playfully. I'm so relieved that it gives me courage. "Tell me. What is this good excuse you have for leaving me sitting here all alone for the past twenty minutes?" I dramatically pout drawing his attention to my lips. Chills run up my spine as he proceeds to run his tongue across his own.

"Well, there really isn't any excuse good enough to keep *you* waiting."

His mouth pulls into a mischievous grin as the intensity of his gaze pushes an image of our naked bodies, tangled and drenched in sweat, to the forefront of my mind. When he sweeps his eyes across my collar bone, I can almost feel his fingers touching me. My breath begins to quiver, so deep in his trance, I can feel the heat rising to my tender parts as my skin prickles deliciously. I want to lean across the table and take his soft, full lips between my teeth.

"I'm glad you know that." My voice is hoarse with desire. I lean in closer, my fingers seductively resting on the stem of my glass. "I hate to be kept waiting."

He's not saying a word, but his message still crosses the space between us. It's in the weight of his gaze, in the hungry way he's watching me. I grip the edge of the table, trying to keep myself from reaching out and tearing his clothes off right here in the middle of the restaurant. Nothing would make me happier.

I take a long, drawn-out sip of my wine, praying my need for him hasn't exposed my hand completely. I taste the plum and oak swirl across my tongue, smooth like crushed velvet. It transforms into an invitation to my place, which sits on my lips begging to be set free. But before I have a chance to make a proposal, Ramtin grabs the menu, creating a partition between us.

"What looks good," he asks.

He diverts all of his attention to the words on the page before him, leaving me feeling cold where there was just heat. The confusion rams into me knocking me back into the moment. As quickly as his advances are made, he reclaims them. His burn fizzles and the desire dissipates, leaving me desperate and wanting.

"No, but seriously, I'm truly sorry for my tardiness. There was a bit of drama with Yasi that I had to attend to. You know how teenagers can be."

"It's okay," I say, downing half my drink.

I feel like an idiot. Here I thought his delay had something to do with me. I half expect him to pull a rose out from behind his back. Isn't that what men his age do? Aren't they part of that forgotten era of chivalry? It's my own fault, really. Letting my hopes build each time he throws a little flirtation my way. Maybe I'm just getting it all wrong but am too naïve to see it. Or it's possible I just don't want to?

He doesn't provide any further explanation of the drama, and I don't bother asking, not interested in what the current teenage dilemma refers to. I'm too preoccupied with this hot and cold dance we've been tangled in all month, to worry about the status of his home front. Irritation boils through my veins. I don't know how much more of this nonsense I can take.

"Are you hungry?" he asks.

"Yeah. Sure," I huff.

Disappointment presses me into the back of my chair like bricks tied to my legs as I'm pulled beneath the ocean. *This is such a waste of my time!* I want more. But every time I think we get closer to the possibility of something, anything more than what we are right now, he shatters it all to hell.

The waitress walks up to the table to take our order.

"Can I get a dirty martini, please?" Wine isn't going to cut it. I need something stronger before I burn a hole into the seat with my frustration.

Ramtin ignores my obvious disappointment as he carries on random conversation. He talks about our hikes and we discuss new trails to attempt. He tells me about work and asks me about mine. I answer, trying desperately to keep the anger out of my voice. Even if I'm not successful, he doesn't act like he notices. I'm not entirely sure that's not worse.

We order food and more drinks. He slowly sips scotch on the rocks, every now and then eyeing me in a way that makes me want to scream and swoon all at the same time. I try to pretend I don't feel goosebumps rise on my flesh or the need yearning inside me to be near him. And when he walks me to the parking lot, I barely look at him, wanting to put distance between us before the void in the middle of my chest swallows me whole.

"Thanks for dinner." I rummage through my purse looking for my keys as he stands patiently beside me. The gentleman in him won't allow him to leave until I'm nestled safely in the driver's seat. I exhale when I finally find them, wanting badly to go.

"Bye, Ramtin."

I take a step toward my door but feel his hand grab my wrist and stop me. I turn and look up at him, swallowing past the lump that's forming in my throat. Why does this keep happening? I feel like a lovesick teenager. When he doesn't speak, just pulls me to him, I have to pinch back tears.

He holds me close, my face pressed against his chest, the rhythmic beating of his heart soothing the ache in mine. His scent intoxicates me, and I want to melt into him, to feel our bodies pressed against each other like this, always. I hate him so much right now for making me feel all the things I'm trying to ignore.

He gently runs his hand across my hair and lays a kiss on the crown of my head. I come undone. All the emotions I've tried to keep bottled up and buried, rise to the surface, threatening to eat me alive. I turn my chin up so he's forced to see the storm raging inside me. I know he won't kiss me, but there's a small part of me praying I'm wrong.

"Drive safe, Bita," he says. Then he lets go.

I turn and get into my car without a word. If I try to say anything, it'll rush out in a flurry of tears and disappointment, and I don't want him to witness that. I don't understand any of this, but I'll be damned if I let him see me crumble as he tears apart any hope I still have.

* * *

"What's up with you?" Shiva asks.

"Nothing. It's just been a long week. I'm tired." I don't tell her that I haven't slept for days, thinking of Ramtin and how we left things two weeks ago. Confused and blurry.

"It's more than that," she probes as she takes a sip of her wine. "Is it that guy?"

Her expression tells me there's no point in lying. We've been friends too long and she knows me too well for any fake pretenses.

"I don't want to talk about it."

Before she has a chance to protest, Pouyah approaches our table.

"Hey, Bita. Shiva," he greets us, taking the seat beside me. He throws his arm over the back of my chair and leans in close. "What are you guys talking about? Looks serious." He laughs.

"Nope, not serious. Bita was telling me about how work was this week," Shiva answers. She's good at keeping things to herself, knowing I don't feel like discussing Ramtin's rejection with Pouyah, of all people.

Out at yet another gathering with the same damn crowd. The circles remain constant and the events plentiful. I don't know why I let Shiva talk me into to coming out tonight. All I want to do is get into my pajamas, watch a sappy love story on Netflix, and go to bed. Being all dolled up with some guy draped on me like a bad accessory is not appealing in the least. But that seems to be exactly what I signed up for, as Pouyah leans close to my ear and whispers seductively.

"Want to get out of here?"

Shiva raises an eyebrow in my direction as she watches Pouyah hit on me. I take a sip of my drink, buying time to come up with a good excuse. I'm in no mood for a sordid rendezvous this evening.

My gaze wanders toward the front of the bar just as Ramtin walks in. He's with another gentleman, bearing a distinct resemblance to him. They share the same dark features and chiseled jawline. However, where his hair is sprinkled with gray, his counterpart's is jet black and uninterrupted. He looks like a younger version of Ramtin.

I don't notice Pouyah twisting a strand of my hair around his fingers as he rests his palm against my shoulder, pulling me in close, until our bodies touch. I don't hear his laughter as he jokes with Shiva, or the greeting he exchanges with Maral when she sits down beside us. All I see is Ramtin, and as he turns, I realize he sees me too.

A smile stretches across his face until he sees Pouyah sitting beside me, and it stops short of reaching its full magnificence. He doesn't falter, just heads over in my direction. I have to consciously keep myself from shoving Pouyah across the room and bolting for the door.

I bailed on our hike last Saturday, feigning a cold. And when he tried to reach out and see how I was doing, I ignored his calls. I needed distance he wasn't giving me. The ups and downs have become unbearable and literally nauseating. I need to get my bearings before I tackle this "friendship" again. Or ever, for that matter. Seems pointless, really. What do I want with a forty-three-year-old friend? Nothing. I have enough friends, evident in the crowd now surrounding this pub table.

Before I have a chance to blink, he's standing beside me and I'm paralyzed by his proximity.

"Hi, Bita."

The table falls silent as I try to find my tongue. I swallow past the dry, graveling throat I'm now nursing.

"Hey, Ramtin."

His eyes sweep across the crowd and settle on Pouyah a moment longer than the rest of my companions.

"How are you? You feeling better?"

"I'm good, thanks. Much better."

The guy that came in with him steps up beside him.

"This is my brother, Kian," he introduces. Brother. Makes sense. They look like twins. "Kian, this is Bita."

"Hi," Kian says, reaching out to shake my hand. He's bubbly and pleasant, oblivious to the tension building between his brother and me. "Hey, everyone," he adds, waving at the table.

"Hi, Kian. I'm Shiva." My best friend suddenly inserts herself into the conversation.

Oh, hell, all I need is for Shiva to end up with Ramtin's brother. Wouldn't that just be brilliant?

"Why haven't you returned my calls?" Ramtin asks. He doesn't seem to care that we have an audience. Or that one in particular is currently invading my personal space. *His confidence is so sexy.*

"Because you're old," Pouyah whispers in my ear. I pull away, batting him from me. *Asshole.*

Hurt crosses his expression but he's too cool to let me make him look like a fool, so he brushes it off and turns his back toward me, striking up a conversation with the other side of the table. A smirk pulls at the corner of Ramtin's lips.

"I've just been busy," I answer.

"Oh. Okay. Are we good for our hike this week?" His expression reminds me of a child waiting for his mother's approval. How ironic that I'd be the parent in this scenario.

"Sure." I plan on bailing again, but I don't want to get into that conversation with so many people watching.

"Cool." An excitement claims his features, causing the hole in my chest to widen. Sadness consumes me. I wish for so much more between us that it hurts. "Have a good time tonight," he adds. "Come on, Kian."

"It was nice meeting you," Kian says to Shiva, who's been chatting his ear off this entire time. I glare at her. *Traitor.* She just winks. "Nice to meet you too, Bita." Well-mannered men are in abundance in this family.

They head over to the other side of the bar, where booths are located, and settle in the far back corner out of sight. I glance toward Pouyah, who is now engaged in a heated conversation with a tall blonde I don't recognize. I don't spare him a second thought; he's of no consequence at the moment.

"Shots," I demand, grabbing Shiva's hand and dragging her toward the bar. "Now."

"Okay!" She steps up beside me obediently.

"Two vodka shots please," she tells the bartender. "Better make that four," she corrects, after glancing at the scowl on my face.

"This isn't funny," I whine.

"I know. But what's the deal, anyway? Do you really dig this guy?

He's nice and all, but he's so...*old*." She emphasizes old as if he's got some incurable STD.

"Ugh, I know." I drop my head into my hands. "I don't know why I'm so bent out of shape, but I really like him. I'm not even sure what it is about him. I'm just drawn to him," I groan. "I haven't felt this way before."

"So, what's the holdup, then?" The bartender drops the shots in front of us and Shiva hands him her card. She slides two over to me.

Kian walks up to the opposite side of the bar and orders drinks, then casually leans against its edge. Shiva flashes him her best "come get me" smile and unnecessarily plays with her hair. Why can't I go for a guy like Kian? He's younger, much closer to our age. Plus, he looks just as good. Not that I'd go for his brother but judging from the way Shiva is fondling him with her eyes, he's off-limits anyway. He winks and raises his glass in her direction before heading back to his booth with their drinks.

"Now, he's hot," she announces, returning her attention to me. "How old do you think he is?"

"No idea. It's the first I'm seeing him. Matter of fact, I don't really know much about Ramtin, if I'm honest. Which doesn't explain why I like him so much. What is wrong with me?"

"Nothing. He's a nice guy. I can admit there's a very appealing energy about him. Besides, matters of the heart never make much sense." She clinks her shot glass against mine. "Bottoms up, my friend." We throw the first round back, followed by the second in close succession.

"One more," I command, as the bartender gets in earshot. He gives me a look that says, weighing in at a buck fifteen, I may want to slow it down. I just wave my hand in the air shooing away his silent warning. He doesn't protest, grabbing the vodka bottle and filling two of the empty glasses in front of us.

"Oh, we're really trying to forget about Ramtin tonight, aren't we?" Shiva teases.

"Shut up," I order. "Just drink. We'll Uber home."

An hour later, the lights overhead have blurred into a tail of red, flashing as I spin on the dance floor. The music is loud, pulsing against my feet as it travels up my spine, numbing the thoughts in my head. I no longer have any idea why I was so upset in the first place. *Mission accomplished.*

As I swirl to the music, I feel two warm hands wrap around my waist and pull me in close. I look up from beneath hooded lids and get a fuzzy image of Pouyah's predatory grin staring down at me. My stomach rolls, but I push it away. I don't want to stop dancing.

He takes my lack of reaction to mean consent and pulls me even closer. He grinds his body against mine and I'm vaguely aware of his hard arousal against my thigh. I smirk to myself, content that I can still turn someone on.

I push off his body and spin, feeling the cold breeze of the air conditioner find my face. It's so hot among all these packed bodies. Sweat drips down my chest, nestling between my breast. I can feel droplets dampening the back of my shirt, but I'm so carefree in the moment, I don't think about how my white top is wet and stuck to my chest, no doubt showing off my pretty lace bra. I just keep bouncing and swaying to the music.

Pouyah's arms find me again and I feel his hard chest against mine. He runs his hand gently down my face pressing a strand of damp hair behind my ear. My brain is sluggish with alcohol, muting the voice of Rational Bita in my head, urging me to pull away before I'm stuck in a moment I don't want to be in. But it's too late. Before I know what's happening, his lips are on mine as he presses his tongue into my mouth. It takes a moment for me to realize what's going on before I push against him trying to dislodge my body from his.

He's built like a tank and I make no headway. I shove harder, contemplating a knee to the groin, when I finally get his attention. He's startled by my protest, his gaze settling on my face with confusion.

"Stop," I demand. He can't hear me over the sound of the music but he's reading my lips because the confusion transforms to anger.

"Are you serious?" he answers. His brows pinch together, and his breathing becomes labored, as his fury balances on the edge. Unconsciously, I take a step back, trying to put some distance between us so we can both cool down.

"Pouyah, we're just friends. That's all."

I turn to leave but his hand is on my wrist in record time. I remind myself that we've both been drinking and neither of us is rational nor fully coherent now. I'm trying to cut him some slack, but when he squeezes to keep me locked into place as I try to wiggle free, rage courses through my veins. *Who does this asshole think he is?*

"Let go of my fucking arm, Pouyah!" We're capturing the attention of the dancers closest to us. I have no idea where my friends are, but none of them are close enough to come to my aid.

Before he has a chance to protest, I feel a strong hand rest on my wrist pulling Pouyah's hand off mine.

"You heard her. Let her go." Ramtin's voice bellows across the dance floor despite the volume of the music. His posture leaves little room for interpretation. I'm convinced that if Pouyah steps up to him, an all-out brawl will ensue.

The strength he exudes as his eyes lock in on his target, and the protective way he steps in front of me, makes my heart race. Other than my brother, no one has ever made me feel as safe as he does when he's around. It's as if I belong to him, but not in the childish, possessive way the men of my generation interpret, but with the respectful, mature understanding that I'm my own person, an independent woman who should be cherished and taken care of when I deem necessary. This moment just confirms how badly I want him in my life.

"What the hell?" Pouyah looks around, realizing we now have an audience watching and the muscles in his jaw tense. His young, hot Persian pride can't take an ego beating so he puffs up his chest and adds, "Are you her father or something, old man?"

Ramtin takes a slow, intimidating step toward Pouyah. His hand is still gripping Pouyah's wrist and I can see his fingers tighten. In a low growl that only the three of us can hear, he warns, "I advise you to walk away. The lady said to leave her alone, so you should do that. If you fail to listen, I'll show you just how much of an old man I really am."

He has a menacing glare in his expression, almost as if he's daring Pouyah to start something. He's a few inches taller, and something in the way Ramtin's body is coiled, cobra-like and tight, screams danger. Pouyah reads it as well, taking a step back as Ramtin releases his wrist.

"Ah, whatever. She's a cock-tease anyway," he declares, as if he couldn't care less.

I exhale, not realizing I've been holding my breath. A smile begins to form on my face before Ramtin turns his gaze on to me. The anger chiseled into his features is plain as day. The elation that he was about to fight for my honor disappears into the nauseating flashing lights.

"Let's go. I'm taking you home." There's no arguing with the demand in his tone.

"Shiva came with me. She's staying at my house," I mumble, knowing that putting up a fight would be useless. Plus, I want to leave. It's only a matter of time before this story spreads across the crowd of my Persian acquaintances. I don't feel like dealing with the scrutiny that is sure to follow.

Kian appears suddenly out of thin air with Shiva tucked beneath his arm. Judging from her droopy lids and enamored grin, she's as drunk as I am. The two men walk us both to the exit and out into the parking lot.

"What about my car?"

"Give me your keys. I'll drive your car to your house while Kian takes mine."

Once the valet brings both our vehicles over, his expression softens as he nestles me into the passenger seat and helps me fasten my seatbelt. We drive home in silence. My head bounces as I struggle to stay awake but fail miserably.

He gently shakes me when we arrive.

"You're home," he whispers. His hot breath spreads across my cheek.

I want to tell him how I feel about him, let him know that I want more. I want to convince him that we could be magnificent. But I can't make my mouth obey my mind. I feel so tired, my brain wading through a pool of molasses, the moments fleeting and out of my grasp.

He puts his arm around me and walks me to my front door, unlocking it and taking me inside. Kian is a few steps behind doing the same with Shiva. They take us over to my room and help us take off our shoes. I direct Ramtin to where I have a stack of oversize t-shirts in my drawer, and he brings two over for us. Kian waits in the living room as Ramtin closes his eyes and drops his head, holding up the comforter while waiting for Shiva and me to stumble out of our clothes and into our makeshift pajamas. Once we climb into bed, he throws the blanket on top of us.

Shiva curls around her pillow and is instantly asleep. I can hear the deepening of her breath as I fight to stay awake. My eyes are closed but I hear Ramtin's footsteps make their way to the bedroom door.

"Sleep well, sweet Bita," I think I hear him say. But I can't be sure.

I'm halfway into the land of dreams when I hear the click of the front door.

* * *

I startle awake, my head aching and my vision spinning. My throat feels parched and I swallow hard against the sandpaper choking me. It takes me a moment before the events of the night come crashing into memory.

Dread seeps into my veins as I recall getting drunk at the bar. The altercation with Pouyah comes into view and the regret and guilt become steel weighing down my insides. My stomach rolls with nausea. I can't tell if it's from the recollection of Pouyah's tongue in my mouth, or all the alcohol I consumed. Either way, I'm running to the bathroom, making it with only seconds to spare before I puke into the toilet.

I sit with my head against the cool bathroom tiles trying to piece the night together. I remember Ramtin and Kian showing up at the same bar and talking to them. I recall taking entirely way too many vodka shots. And I remember dancing with Pouyah until he decided to make-out with me. Bits and pieces begin to fall into place as Ramtin's face appears, threatening Pouyah with his quite strength. Then I remember them driving us home.

Shiva is still asleep, hair tangled across her face, her arm hanging off the side of my bed. Her breath whistles on the exhalation, creating its own little repetitive melody. I close the bedroom door and head to the kitchen.

I walk straight to the coffee pot and turn it on. Thank God; I'd set it the night before. I need caffeine as badly as I need air right now. I just stare at it dripping slowly into the pot and decide I need a faster coffee maker. Once it's finally complete and I have a mug of hot steamy joe in my hand, I turn to sit at the table.

Positioned in the center are both my purse and Shiva's. They're sitting side by side, but they're not what catches my attention. Folded neatly and nestled between them is a piece of paper. From this distance, I can see the shadow of black ink marks. I make it to the table in two big strides, forgetting about the vicious hangover I'm nursing. I snatch the note and stare at Ramtin's writing across the front.

Inside he's scrawled a message in his architecturally perfect penmanship.

Bita,
   I hope you're feeling better this morning. Call me if you need anything.
   Love,
   Ramtin

I run my fingers over the indents left behind by his pen as embarrassment from the night before chokes me. I let out a groan. *He must think I'm such an immature idiot!* I suddenly want to cry.

I can't imagine how I looked to him on the dance floor, twirling like a moron, then in the clutches of Pouyah as he rammed his tongue down my throat. I'm paralyzed thinking that I've taken the little chance I had left with Ramtin and threw it out the window. I can't let that be the last image he has of me, even if he's done dealing with my shenanigans.

I burst into motion, running around the house brushing my teeth while simultaneously getting dressed. I don't even bother with makeup or doing my hair. I just let it whip around my face, flat and lifeless, as I grab my keys and head out the door.

Fifteen minutes later, I'm standing in front of Ramtin's home. He pointed it out to me in passing on the way back from the coffee shop a few weeks ago. I know my showing up unexpectedly, to a house I've never been to, could appear very stalker-ish, but I don't care. I'm functioning on pure adrenaline, terrified I may have lost Ramtin for good.

I don't let my common sense take over, flying up the steps and ringing his bell. It takes a few minutes before a bleary-eyed Ramtin swings the door open.

"Bita? Are you okay?"

I whip my wrist up and look at the time on my watch. *Oh, God, it's six-thirty in the morning! Why didn't I check that before I headed over here like a maniac? Kill me now!*

"Oh my God." I cover my mouth with my hand, trying to suppress the groan pushing its way across my tongue. "I'm so sorry, I didn't realize how early it was!" I'm mortified.

He rubs his eyes. "It's okay. But are you okay? Why are you here?"

I just stare at him for a few seconds, speechless. Why am I here? What did I come here to prove? That I'm worth it? Shouldn't he know that already? I almost turn and walk away without a word.

He pushes the door open and steps aside. "Come in," he says. The kindness in his expression causes my heart to constrict and tears threaten to pool in my lids. I try to grab hold of the little resolve I have left.

Once we're in his living room, he asks, *"Chayee meekhaye? Do you want tea?"*

"No, thanks." I shake my head. I'm uncertain of what to say. I want so badly to start over, begin the night again but give it an alternate ending. I follow him into the kitchen because sitting on the couch, alone, in this unfamiliar house, seems too depressing.

He sits across from me at the table.

"How are you feeling?" he asks, grinning. The tension eases ever so slightly from my shoulders.

"Ramtin, I'm so sorry," I blurt out.

"For what?"

"For being a drunk idiot last night and for having you witness all of it." I drop my gaze to my hands intertwined on the wooden surface. If the floor could open up and swallow me whole right now, I'd let it.

"You didn't do anything wrong," he assures me. "You just had a little too much to drink. We've all been there." He reaches out and squeezes my hand. He lets his fingers rest on top of mine. The feel of his rough palms reminds me of a love affair we haven't yet had, but one that I dreamt of often.

"I'm sorry about Pouyah."

He looks away. A flash of anger crosses his face, but he doesn't say a word. He goes to pull his hand from mine, but I grab hold.

"What are we doing?" I ask. He doesn't look at me. Just keeps staring out the window. "I don't understand. One minute you're hot, the next you're cold. I'm so confused, and I just can't take it anymore."

"There's nothing going on with us, Bita. We're just friends." He returns his gaze to my face and slowly pulls his hand away. I wonder if he can feel me teetering on the edge of heartbreak, each word a dagger through my chest.

"But why?" My voice is hoarse as I struggle to maintain control. Again, he doesn't speak. "I don't understand. I know you feel what I feel. I can see it. Or am I misinterpreting it all? Maybe I'm a fool to think you have feelings for me, too."

His lids tighten, hiding the brilliance of his eyes behind his pain. His lips struggle to form words, but then he gives up, sighing heavily with defeat.

"Talk to me," I beg.

"We can't be more than friends, Bita."

"I don't understand."

"I'm so much older than you. Our lives are in different places. You're just starting yours, and I'm already halfway through mine."

I reach out and grab his hand, resting limply before him. "I don't care about the age difference," I insist.

He gently untangles our fingers placing his hand in his lap. "Well, you should," he urges. "And even if that wasn't an issue, which it is, my life is complicated. I have daughters to think about. I need to focus on them right now."

"I'd never come between you and your daughters."

"I know you wouldn't, but they need me. All of me. Not just bits and pieces of my attention. I don't know how to explain it, but I haven't always been the father they need, and I really can't let them down again."

I can hear him telling me this isn't going to work, but his pained expression gives me pause. He rubs his jaw, pulling the inside of his cheek between his teeth in hesitation. I can't suppress the hope that tickles my insides.

"How can you walk away from this, from us, when you know it could be so amazing?" I ask.

He stares at me, opening his mouth to speak, then decides otherwise. The weight of his words unsaid chips away at my resolve. Then he turns his gaze back to the window, shutting me out. In his silence, I get my answer. With the little strength I have left I stand, letting his hand drop to the table. If he wanted this, he would say it.

I turn and slowly make my way toward the door, telling myself to put one foot in front of the other. So much disappointment fills me that I feel like my body weighs a ton. I knew I wanted this, but until this moment, I hadn't realized just how much.

I reach out to grab the door handle, but I feel Ramtin's arm on my shoulder swinging me around to face him. I stare bewildered, trying to find my tongue, to say all the words wrapped up in my frustration. But the gentleness in his eyes stills my heart. He places his hands on either side of my face, the heat from his fingers burning my skin with longing. Slowly, he leans in, balancing his lips so close to mine that when he speaks, I can feel his breath.

"We shouldn't do this," he warns, the words escaping in a painful groan.

I stop breathing, certain he's about to turn away. But before the dismay begins to tighten its fingers around my lungs, he leans in and kisses me.

It starts soft and timid, almost as if he's asking permission. From me, from himself, or maybe the relationship gods, to move forward, to embark on this journey of hope and love with me. Then, as I press my body to his, he moves a hand into my hair and holds me close, his tongue asking for passage. I grant him access to my mouth, my body, my soul.

He kisses me softly and deeply, building until the need to feel my core interlocked with his devours me. I put my arms around his neck, stand on my tiptoes, and melt into him.

I'm suddenly airborne. He carries me, as if I weigh nothing more than a feather, into his bedroom and places me gently on the bed. His body hovers over mine and I pull his shirt up over his head. I rip mine off as well, lying beneath him half naked. His eyes run over my skin, the bare flesh of my stomach, my breast, my neck, where he nuzzles his head and draws circles with his tongue.

His touch is smooth and fluid, a continuous teasing of all my senses, until I feel that I may shatter into a million pieces beneath him. The rest of our clothes are discarded onto the floor in between each fingertip that grazes over my body.

He looks down on me with desire so deep it mimics the vast ocean. So many secrets lay hidden beneath the surface, all calling to me like a siren in the night. I hook my legs around his waist and pull him down to me, no longer able to stand the distance between us. When he enters inside me, I burst into flames, igniting the walls around us.

Each thrust brings me closer to the edge, one I've visited before, but never like this. His expert hands know how to touch me, to fill my insides with passion and need, to take me to the brink of my demise and hold me steady until I'm made of nothing but my emotions. And when he brings himself to meet me, we crash and burn into the sheets in unison.

As I lay with my legs draped over him, while he soothingly runs his hand through my hair, I wonder how many other females he's touched like this. The idea that I'm not the first to have him look at me with the yearning I can clearly see in his gaze breaks my heart. I've never wanted to be someone's one and only. Not until now.

CHAPTER SIX

"So, you going to spill or what?" Sara asks.

She's sitting cross-legged on my couch, balancing a hot cup of *chayee* between her fingertips, waiting. I really don't want to tell her about me and Ramtin. It's been two glorious months since the morning that changed it all, and I won't let my family ruin it for me.

Sara won't be against it. She's cool. But I don't know if she can keep a secret and if she tells my nosy brother, he'll surely have questions. And opinions. Ones I'm certain I won't like hearing.

Despite being younger and modern, Maziar has an old Iranian man streak, as if he were plunged into this world with bits of a past life he can't shake. Especially when it comes to me. I have no idea why I'm such a sensitive topic for him, but he's always been protective. Add Mom's disdain, which will undoubtedly follow the news, and it's a recipe for a war—one I'm not interested in engaging in.

"Come on! Why won't you tell me?" she whines. "I'm dying over here."

I laugh, stretching out on the opposite couch and shake my head.

"I can't tell you."

"Why?" she pouts.

"That doesn't work on me. Just my brother," I tease.

She throws a pillow across the room and I giggle, catching it before it hits my head.

"Okay, but why won't you tell me? You tell me everything else." She has a point. Which is amazing, considering where we started, hating each other and wanting nothing more than to demolish the other's existence.

"Because," I answer, now also in a whiny voice. "You'll tell my brother and I don't feel like dealing with him."

"I won't tell him," she assures me.

"Liar."

"I promise. Just tell me. I'm dying to know what's going on with you two. And don't say 'nothing.' I know something is. It was obvious when I saw you guys together months ago and it's obvious in the way you're blushing right now." There's no judgment in her giddiness, only pure curiosity. It makes me smile, and no matter how hard I try, I can't stop.

Thoughts of Ramtin instantly bring on the flutter of rapid butterfly wings in my chest. I'm so happy—ecstatic, really—that I've found the possibility of my own Happily Ever After. I want nothing more than to scream it from the rooftops or at least share it with those I love. Keeping it a secret may cause me to combust.

As I stare at Sara's deep brown eyes, filled with so much hope and excitement for me, I hear myself say, "Okay, what do you want to know?"

I just want to share my news with someone who I know will at least be on my side. Sara understands firsthand how tough a struggle with my family can be. She gets that my apprehension is forcing me to keep it quiet. For now, anyway.

"Everything!" she demands. "Start from the beginning when you were house hunting,"

About an hour later, I've recalled every detail that's led Ramtin and me to our current state of being, while tirelessly answering all the questions Sara interjects along the way. She leans back on the couch, a throw pillow clutched against her chest, and sighs.

"You're acting like *you* just started a new relationship," I giggle.

"I just love the beginnings. They're so amazing, all passion and nerves."

"Are you trying to say you don't feel butterflies with Maziar anymore?"

"No, of course I do. I love him. It's just different. That element of the unknown, when no big commitments have been made. Not that you guys aren't committed or anything," she adds, her hands raised in caution. "But you know what I mean. You're just starting, and everything is so new and fresh. It's the best time." She dreamily gazes through the living room window. But then her expression darkens, worry pressing down on her before she turns back to face me. "When are you going to tell the family?"

"Ugh," I groan, putting my own pillow over my face and hiding. As if that will solve my problems. "I don't know. I really like him, Sara. But it's complicated." I turn to face her so the pillow is balancing on the side of my face. "I don't want to tell them. They'll just mess it up."

"What do you mean, it's complicated?"

"He's really worried about the age gap between us. Like he's messing up my life somehow by being so old."

"I mean, he's older, but he's not *that* old," she points out.

"Right! That's what I said. But he's doesn't agree. And then there's the whole divorce thing."

"He's divorced?" Sara's nose crinkles with the news.

"Yeah," I confirm. I pause, gathering courage before I add, "And he has two daughters."

"Oh." I cringe at Sara's wide-eyed reaction.

"That's not the worst part. His oldest is closer to my age than he is."

"Well, that is a bit of a predicament, isn't it?" Sara's concerned expression makes me uneasy. She's the most compromising of my family members. If she appears apprehensive about my new relationship, I don't want to know what the others will think.

"But none of that matters. Not really, anyway. So, he's older. Who cares? And yeah, he has daughters, but it'll be fine. I know it will." I nod to myself, hoping that's enough of a confirmation for the universe. "It's been such a struggle to get him to let his guard down and actually listen to his feelings." I try to pinch back the tears that have suddenly sprung to my eyes.

"Is he not sure that he wants this?" Sara asks.

"He does," I say. "But, at the same time, he's hesitant. Even if he won't admit it, I can still see moments when he questions our decision to be together. I don't know how to convince him that I'm not losing anything by choosing to be with him." I sit back up so I'm facing Sara again. "I don't want to tell my family about us because if they aren't on our side, I'm terrified it will break us."

She watches me for a moment, understanding crossing her features.

"I'm sorry, honey," she offers. I mean you can keep it a secret for a while, I guess, but they'll eventually find out, Bita. You know that. Someone will see you and somehow it will get back to your brother or your mom. You know how small the community can feel. Wouldn't it be better if you told them before that happens?" Always the voice of reason.

"I know," I answer. "I just wish I didn't have to tell them at all."

* * *

"I'm so hungry," Ramtin announces.

He pulls open the café door for me to walk through. I run my hand across his chest as I pass, the need to physically feel him ever present. He steps beside me and wraps his arm around my waist as we make our way over to the counter.

We've just finished our workout, opting to go to the gym today, neither in the mood for the outdoors. We were up late last night, watching movies and eating junk food on my couch, and couldn't make the early rise.

My mind is groggy from the lack of sleep, and I don't think to scan the room as I usually do. Living so close to home always poses the risk of running into someone I know. I tend to pick locations I'm sure my parents would never frequent, but still. I don't realize my rookie mistake until I hear my brother from a table to the left.

"Bita?"

Dread launches into my throat at the sound of Maziar's voice. *Crap!*

I do my best to stay calm, but my body reflexively tightens. Ramtin's expert observation skills alert him to my discomfort. He whips his head in my direction, having been busy looking at the menu.

"What's wrong?"

There's no time for me to answer before Maziar is standing before us, catching Ramtin's attention.

"Hey, Maziar." Ramtin extends his hand to my brother.

Maziar accepts the handshake and I exhale...until my brother's gaze traces Ramtin's arm around my waist, and I stop breathing again. When he looks at me, there's confusion and anger burning in his eyes. I have no idea if he's pissed about the fact that I'm with Ramtin or that he didn't know. I'm hoping this is one of those "why didn't you tell me" sibling issues, but judging from his death glare, I'm thinking it's the former.

"What are you guys doing here?" Maziar asks.

The casual way he grins and engages as he directs his attention to Ramtin only puts me further on edge. It's all a ruse, one I have a feeling will explode into shrapnel the first time he gets me alone. I have to consciously force myself to stand tall and not allow his strength to override my own.

I'm an adult. I'm the older sibling. He doesn't get to have a say.

I repeat it in my head as I meet his fury with my own. Sara is on her feet and stationed beside us. She lovingly drapes her arm through Maziar's, appearing like the newlyweds that they are. I wonder though if she's getting a grip so she can hold him back if the two of us decide to take our battle of wills to the next level. We aren't the fist-fighting type, but at this moment, I would really love to punch that smug look off my brother's face.

"We came to get some food," I say.

"We just got back from the gym. Tough workout," Ramtin adds. The disapproval emanating off my brother doesn't faze him. He stays calm and collected as always.

"Working out and having lunch. I didn't even realize you two were hanging out."

"We are." I meet Maziar's cockiness with my own.

"Hmmm," he replies, staring straight at me.

I can see Ramtin watching us, quietly analyzing the exchange. I'll have some explaining to do. We haven't really talked about who I've told so far. He knows Shiva is aware of our relationship because she's gone out with us a few times. She's got the hots for Kian, which makes her the best partner in crime. But we haven't discussed if my family knows. It's obvious now that they don't.

I'm not sure how he's going to react after this encounter, but I'm praying this doesn't send him back into another tailspin where he pulls away and clams up.

"It was so great to see you guys," Sara interjects. "But we have to get some errands done and we were just finishing up." She steps in between Maziar and I and gives me a hug. "See you later?"

"Yeah," I reply, squeezing her. She locks eyes with me as she pulls away and gives me a reassuring nod, silently letting me know she'll do damage control. I can always count on her. "Come on, Maziar. Let's go."

Maziar turns toward Ramtin and finds his manners. "It was great seeing you, man. Now that you're hanging with my sister, maybe we can all go out sometime. Get to know each other better."

"Sure. I'd love that," Ramtin says.

"Bye, Sis." He leans in and hugs me. "We need to talk," he whispers in my ear.

The weight of his words lace through my limbs coiling my muscles tight. I want to tell him to keep the news to himself before blabbing it to Mom and Dad, so we can discuss it, but he lets go too quickly for any more words to be exchanged. My stomach knots in frustration.

I watch them walk out of the café doors and down the street. Maziar throws his arm around Sara, and she laces her fingers with his. *Why can't he just stick to his Happily Ever After? Why does he have to mess with mine? Didn't what he and Sara had to go through teach him anything?*

"Well, that was interesting." Ramtin pulls my attention back to him.

"Sorry." I don't know what else to say.

"It's to be expected, I guess," he replies. It doesn't take a genius to put the pieces together. A twenty-eight-year-old dating a man fifteen years her senior, who's divorced with two kids, isn't exactly what every parent dreams of. Especially Iranian ones.

Ramtin turns toward the counter, focusing on the line of people ahead of us. He's taken his arm away from my waist and a step to his right to create space.

"Don't do that," I demand, closing the distance. I wrap my arm around him instead and pull him into me.

"Do what?" he asks, staring down at me with his beautifully concerned expression. Even in this worried state, when his features are pinched together, he takes my breath away.

"Pull away from me and convince yourself this is a mistake. It's taken us too much effort to get here, to be with each other. Don't let my brother's small-mindedness ruin that."

"It's not just your brother. What about your parents? You don't think they're also going to have a problem with this? Of course they will. Hell, I even might if it were my daughter. You're young. I'm not. It's just the facts. You should be having fun, not dealing with battles."

"I am having fun," I protest.

"You know what I mean, Bita. This is going to be a miserable fight when your parents find out. I'm almost twice your age. It makes more sense for me to be your father rather than your boyfriend."

"Boyfriend?" I ask, raising a brow.

I'm hoping my playfulness eases the tension, but he just smiles wearily at me and gently kisses my forehead. I get the eerie sense he's saying goodbye.

"Wipe that sad look off your face. No one is saying goodbye today," I demand. "You let me worry about my family. I can handle them." I'm not certain whether I'll get through to them, but I know I won't leave Ramtin.

He shakes his head at me and grins. "You're so stubborn."

"Damn straight I am. It would do you good to realize that sooner rather than later," I tease. Then I stand on my tiptoes and kiss him.

His hand finds the small of my back and pulls me closer. I wrap my arms around his neck, getting lost in the feel of him, with little regard for who's watching. Here, in this spot, in the middle of our favorite café, a little piece of my own personal heaven exists. It's the most fabulous thing I've ever experienced, and I refuse to lose it. I won't. Not for my brother or my parents.

I've finally found what it is I didn't even realize I'd been looking for, and now that I have, I know with certainty that I'm willing to risk it all.

* * *

"How old were you when you came to the United States?" I ask.

My head is on Ramtin's chest, my fingers playing with the tiny tuft of hair nestled in the valley of his breastbone. The black and gray strands twist together in inconsistent waves, creating patches of light and dark. His heart thrums against my ear, my own soothing lullaby. He's running his hand across my head, softly pulling my hair between his thumb and forefinger. It lulls me even further into a peaceful state.

"I was eleven," he answers. "We left in 1986."

"Was the war still going on?" History is not my strong suit and I can feel the red creep up my neck in response. I don't want him to think I'm an idiot.

"Yes. The Iran-Iraq war was going on. It didn't end until 1988."

"So, when was the *enghelab, revolution,* everyone talks about? I don't know my dates very well."

"The revolution started in 1979. That's when Ayatollah Khomeini declared Iran as an Islamic republic, when all the strict rules came into play, like the extreme emphasis on woman's dress code. The *roosaries, head scarves,* and *monto, body cover,* became mandatory then."

There's no judgment in the way Ramtin answers my questions. He just feeds my curiosity while we lie blissfully in bed together.

"Was it hard?" I ask. "Being there in the middle of a war, I mean."

"It was," he says. His hand stops mid-caress across my head, alerting me to his discomfort. "It was really hard," he repeats.

I lift up on my elbow so I can look at him. His eyelids are tight with the memories, his lips pulled down in a frown. The pain of his experience is clearly displayed across his face, and I suddenly wish I could go back in time and save him.

"Will you tell me about it?" I ask, my voice a whisper. I'm afraid I may be imposing on something too personal to share. But, as I lie in bed with the man I know I'm falling in love with, naked beneath the sheets, I wonder if anything is too personal.

He turns onto his side, folding his arm beneath his head. I lay back down, facing him, waiting for a story I hope he trusts me enough to tell. I can see him struggle with the images, an uncomfortable scowl claiming his features. I reach out and run my hand along the side of his face, cupping his cheek with my palm.

"Tell me," I urge.

"I was eleven and Kian was four," he begins. "The country was in unrest, the ayatollah having already taken over and the war with Iraq going on. There were sirens and bombings. It was terrifying, especially as a child.

"I remember one night in particular. It was in the early hours of the morning, pitch black outside. Kian and I were sleeping side by side upstairs. The sirens went off, and suddenly the house was shaking. Sadly, we were used to hearing the explosions but rarely did we feel them. On this night, though, the bombs were close, and the house shook like it was an earthquake. I just remember feeling like I had to protect Kian, so I threw myself on top of him, sheltering him with my body. He wouldn't stop screaming. I'll never forget the way he sounded." A sharp intake of breath passes through his lips.

I cringe as the images of the night are painted across my own mind. The fear and uncertainty that Ramtin must have felt knocks the air out of my lungs. I can see him reach out, pulling Kian beneath him and using his body as a shield. The horror seeps into my bones, transporting me into a time I know nothing about.

"I'm sorry," I say, my words lost to war-painted pictures.

He leans in and kisses my forehead. "It's not your fault."

"I know." I drop my gaze to the sheets pooled around his chest. "I just hate that you lived through that."

"Hey," he murmurs, putting his hand beneath my chin until I'm looking at him. "I'm okay," he reassures me.

I pinch back tears. "We grew up hearing stories, but we never really understood it because it just felt so far away and unreal. It breaks my heart that you were there." I run my hand softly down the side of his arm. Goosebumps follow the trail I make, but I don't feel the usual thrill at his physical response to my touch. The war-torn story he's telling overpowers the moment. "Do you still think about it?"

"No, not as much. It was worse when we were younger. Kian would wet his bed until he was almost eleven from the stress of the experience. He had nightmares well into his teenage years. It's a horrible thing for a kid to see."

"I can't imagine."

"I'm glad you don't have to," he replies. "No one should."

"How did you actually get out of the country? They weren't letting anyone leave, right?"

"No, not easily. It was a long process. Everyone was scared for their lives. Even Muslims wanted to escape, afraid their sons would be sent to war. Everyone wanted out." He pauses. "You really want to hear this story?" he asks. "It's not your typical pillow talk." He laughs, but the sound is dark.

"I really want to hear it. It's part of who you are, and I want to know everything there is to know about you. And I should know this. Every Iranian was affected in one way or another."

He watches me for a moment, a decision being made behind his brooding pupils. Then he turns onto his back, grabbing my hand and interlacing his fingers with mine, holding it against his chest as he begins.

"It was hard for anyone to leave the country. It didn't matter who you were. Once the regime changed and the war began, no one could get passports."

He shifts beneath the sheet exposing his chest further. The sun has made its way through the bedroom window, creating a shimmery glow across his skin. If this were any other conversation, I wouldn't be able to resist the desire to lay my lips gently against his body.

"My mom would spend hours every week waiting in lines to just be turned down when she requested passports for us. She was trying to get three, one for her and two for Kian and me. We were supposed to leave first, and then Dad was going to follow."

"Why?" I ask.

"If anyone attempted to get the entire family out, the government would become suspicious that you were trying to escape."

"But why didn't they want anyone to leave?"

"I guess they didn't want the whole country to empty out? I'm not entirely sure. The sons were wanted for war. Everyone had to do time as a solider. Either way, it was horrible," he says. "Anyway, once my parents realized getting passports legally wasn't going to work, they started looking for alternative options. My dad found a guide, like the coyotes that help people cross the border here."

Suddenly, images of people crossing through rough terrain without food and water, like in the movies, consume my thoughts, and my hand flies to my mouth, stifling a gasp.

"What is it?" Ramtin's brows pinch together in concern.

"You had to cross through the desert on foot at eleven?" I stare at him, wide-eyed and enraged by what Little Ramtin had to endure.

"No," he gently assures me. "It was bad, but not like that kind of bad. We didn't backpack or anything."

"So how did you do it?"

"Dad paid the guide to make us four passports. My parents decided they wanted to stay together, and since we weren't getting legal papers, it was just a matter of paying more. But in the end, the guide stole our money and said he couldn't take us."

"What? Are you serious?" I exclaim with incredulity.

"Yeah. My dad was so desperate to get us out. He was terrified for our lives as the war started to make its way into the cities. He'd gone gray in a matter of months, his frame crumpled with despair. He just looked sick."

Ramtin's gaze finds the framed photo of his parents on his nightstand. He reaches over and grabs it, holding it up in front of us. He runs his thumb across his father's picture, nostalgia bouncing off the walls of the bedroom.

"I remember thinking that the entire thing was going to kill him. He was an Iranian man, and even though I never heard him say it, I know he felt incompetent and incapable of protecting us."

We lie in bed for the next hour and a half as Ramtin walks me through his horrific experience. His father finds another man with connections and pays someone to make them fake IDs with a different last name and birthplace. Their given Muslim identities.

"Did that bother them? Having to pretend to be Muslim when they were Jewish?"

"Honestly, no. They just wanted to get us out. And the Muslims weren't to blame. It was just the fanatics that had ruined everything. They were more terrified about being caught."

He continues, telling me his mom returned to the passport department with their fake IDs, praying they wouldn't find out. Finally, after endless attempts, she was told to return in two weeks. What felt like a lifetime later, she went back and was issued four temporary passes.

"We took a bus to Turkey, because it was riskier going by plane. The entire thing was filled with people trying to get out for good, young college students, mothers with their children. Muslims and Jews alike. Many of the husbands were left behind," he says. "My dad's business partner, Reza, couldn't get a pass, so he sent his wife and baby with us."

"Oh, that's so terrible."

"It was. Nasim was like a second mother to me."

"Were they Muslim? Their names are, right?" I ask.

"Yes. As I said, it was difficult for everyone. For some reason, they would only issue passage for her. I watched her hold onto her husband before we got on the bus, sobbing like the world was coming to an end. Even though I was just a child, I could feel the magnitude of the moment. It felt like my heart was going to explode from sadness."

He pauses, stopping to regain control of his shaky voice. I can see fresh tears pooling in his lids, his energy somber with the memory. My lungs burn in response to the anguish he wears.

"I can still vividly see Dad leaning in as he whispered words of comfort to Reza, who was trying desperately to hold it together. But his pain was obvious, his eyes red from the strain of not shedding a tear at his family's departure, and his muscles clenched with his will to maintain control."

As he continues, adding brick by brick to the painfully horrid picture he's painting for me, I'm filled further with despair. My heart breaks for the young child Ramtin was and the fear he must have experienced. The knowledge of his family's story, as well as that of Reza and Nasim, pushes me into the mattress with disbelief.

"I remember my mom and Nasim crying the entire way, quietly into their scarves, holding tightly to each other, after they'd thought we'd all gone to sleep. My mom was leaving her parents and family behind and didn't have any idea when and if she'd ever see them again." A tear escapes his eye and he brushes it away. "God, I miss her."

I snuggle in closer and kiss his shoulder.

His mother passed away years ago when Ramtin was in his early twenties, and I know they had a very strong bond. It makes me think of Mom and what I would do if she were to die. The thought alone sends me into an instant panic.

"The bus stopped in a small city about an hour out from the border. We got out to eat and stretch our legs but then ended up having to sleep in our seats. Somewhere around five in the morning, we were awakened by *sepahee, military guards,* flooding the bus and flashing their lights into our eyes. They made us all pull out our IDs and scrutinized each one, making sure we were all legally crossing into Turkey. Most of us weren't. When one of the guards made his way over to us, I could hardly breathe, terrified we were going to be caught and that they would take us to jail. Or worse." I rub his shoulder, wishing I could wipe away the memories of that night. "I was a kid. I had no idea what would happen if they figured out our IDs were fake."

"That's so awful."

"Yeah. I had to sit on my hands, they were shaking so badly. I remember he stood over us forever, staring at the Ids, then at each of us. Nasim's baby started crying, and he yelled at her to shut him up. She pressed his face into her shoulder as he sobbed, trying to muffle the sound, while she whispered in his ear and comforted him."

My heart slams against my ribcage in unison to the terror conveyed in his words. His nightmare becomes my own as I take each step, hold each breath, along with the younger version of the man lying beside me. No one should ever have to experience what he's been through. And sadly, I realize that there are some that have been through fates far worse.

"Thankfully, everyone on the bus checked out," he says on an exhalation. "We were an hour out from Turkey, so it wasn't long until we got to the border. I remember the moment we stepped onto Turkey's soil, having cleared through customs, all the women took off their *roosaries,* and the men bought food and beer. A full-on celebration began, with childhood songs and dancing around picnic tables. It was an amazing moment for all of us. I think it was the first time I was able to take a full breath in months."

"That must have been such a relief."

"It was. I can't describe the weight that lifted off my dad's shoulders. You could physically see it. He stood just a bit taller that day and the smile finally reached the edges of his eyes." He grins as he recalls his father's reaction. "There still was quite a way to go before we ended up here. We went to Russia, then Switzerland, and finally Italy. Depending on where we were, the living conditions varied. Some good, some not so great."

"That must be so scary for parents, worrying about what will happen not only to them, but their kids, too."

He squeezes my hand, but the mention of children causes the scowl to momentarily resurface. It's Ramtin's standard response to all comments I make that are kid-related. He won't admit it, but I know in my gut that he worries about our future and... children. He's older than I am, and he already has kids, two factors that he's determined will affect me. I've never asked him if he wants more, but from his constant worry about our age difference, I'm wondering if I should.

I'm not sure I even know if I want kids. Or at least that's what I keep telling myself. Truth is, I don't want to lose him. I haven't yet figured out how much I'm willing to sacrifice to keep him in my life.

"We were in Italy for four months before our papers were fixed and we could come to the U.S. But crossing into Turkey was the toughest part," he continues. "If you made it that far then you knew you had at least broken free. We got here in February of 1987."

"Wow, that took a long time."

"About six months."

"Sounds horrible." I tried to imagine six months of uncertainty, of nowhere to call home, nothing to keep my family secure. The displacement would be jarring and literally devastating.

"Did Nasim come with you guys to the United States as well?"

"No, she had family in London, so she headed there."

"Please tell me Reza made it to her," I plead.

"Yes, he did." Ramtin grins as I sigh with relief. "They're still there with their kids. Their daughter is married and has two children of her own, and their son is working on a master's degree now," he recalls fondly. "She calls me once a month to see how Kian and I are doing. When my mother died, she stepped in as her replacement." Thoughts of his surrogate mother brightens his expression. A light at the end of a dusty tunnel. "But that's enough about that," he insists. "I don't want to spend the day depressed." He smirks as he pulls me up until I'm lying on top of him. I giggle, leaning down and kissing his nose.

"Thank you for sharing your story with me."

"I want to share everything with you." His voice is hoarse with emotion. The way he's staring at me causes chills to run up my spine. There's so much hidden in his glance, an abyss of the unknown. I want to reach inside and pull him out before it drowns him beneath its darkness.

"What is it?" I ask.

He doesn't say a word, tangling his fingers through my hair and pulling my lips to his. He kisses me deeply, causing heat to rise through my body, dizzying me with his touch. I forget my momentary concern, the way his expression makes me nervous, and that nagging feeling that he's always preparing himself to say goodbye. Instead, I wrap my body tightly around his and get lost in the moment.

"I love you, Bita," he whispers against my lips.

As the words leave his mouth, my heart bursts into a fury of stars raining down around me. I feel like I'm floating.

"I love you, too."

CHAPTER SEVEN

The doorbell rings multiple times in a row as I step out of the shower. I'm not expecting anybody. It's noon on Saturday, and I don't have plans with Ramtin until later tonight. I hurriedly wrap a towel around my body and rush out to see what the commotion is all about. The bell rings two more times in succession.

"Hold your horses," I complain to no one in particular, as I come running down the hall.

I spy Maziar standing at the front door. *Just fabulous.*

"What took you so long?" he asks, when I open the door. He's wearing an award-winning scowl of frustration. His gaze runs the length of me, taking in my half-naked body, then glances behind me, scanning the room.

"No one's here," I huff. "I was in the shower." I hold up a strand of my wet hair for confirmation, in case the towel doesn't state the obvious. "Did we have plans?"

"Nope." He pushes past me into the living room, carrying two brown paper bags he holds up for me to see. "I just thought I'd bring you lunch."

His childlike grin should be endearing, and on any other given day, this would totally have made me warm and fuzzy inside. Maziar likes to surprise me with food and goodies, always ready for sibling bonding time. But today, a week after catching me at the café with Ramtin, I know he has ulterior motives.

I swing the door shut. "I need to put on some clothes."

"I'll be here when you get back." He winks.

"That's what I'm afraid of," I mumble to myself as I head down the hall.

I put my clothes on as slowly as I can, trying to piece together the various points of my defense. After Ramtin and I ran into my brother, I was determined to have this conversation with Maziar. I wanted to cut him off at the pass before he had a chance to tell my parents about my relationship. But for some reason, I chickened out. I think part of me just didn't want to burst the happy bubble I was living in. And the other part may have been hoping he'd blab, so I wouldn't have to.

Pretending that my family will accept Ramtin with open arms is starting to get harder to believe. And, judging from the annoying man humming away in my living room, greasy peace offering in hand, it appears that the time has come to face the facts.

I love Ramtin, and my family is going to hate it.

I head back out to find Maziar sitting at the table in my kitchen nook, burgers and fries laid out before him, sipping on his fountain drink, while staring out the window. I come up beside him and pause to watch the kids playing outside.

"This is a really nice neighborhood."

Two boys speed down the sidewalk on their bikes.

"Yeah it is. It's peaceful. I love sitting here with my cup of coffee in the morning and just staring out the window. There are always kids playing outside. Reminds me of when we were young." I sigh, nostalgia for my youth more prominent as I age.

I take the seat in front of Maziar and fold my hands in front of me, patiently waiting. He doesn't notice for a moment but then turns to place his soda down and finds me staring.

"What?" he asks. The innocent expression he wears amplifies my irritation. It rattles around in my chest like loose change in a dryer, redundant and annoying.

"Why are you here?" *Let's rip off this Band-Aid.*

"What do you mean? Why do I need to have a reason to hang out with my sister?" he answers. The malicious twinkle in his eye complements the grin stretched across his lips. "I brought you lunch." He points to the food he's placed in front of the seat across from him.

"Cut the shit, Maziar. We both know why you're here. Let's just get this over with," I demand.

He eyes me thoughtfully, then says, "Okay." He leans forward, resting his elbows on the table, placing his chin on his hands. "What are you thinking, Bita? What are you doing with this guy?"

"His name is Ramtin. Have enough courtesy to give him an identity. And as for what I'm doing with him, I'm dating him."

"But why him? He's too old for you."

"He's not that much older," I protest.

"He's forty-five?"

"Forty-three," I correct him.

"Okay, so that's fifteen years. You're trying to tell me you couldn't find a guy closer to your age than that?"

"What does that even matter?" I exhale, trying to steady my nerves. A screaming match won't get us anywhere. Plus, if I can coerce Maziar onto my side, it will help when I deal with the parental units.

"It's not ideal. But that's not the only problem. Take into consideration that he's a real estate agent, divorced, and has kids. The cons are stacked against him." Apparently, Maziar was paying attention when Dad asked Ramtin about himself before we hired him on as our agent.

"Oh my God, could you sound anymore like Mom right now? When did you become so damn uptight?" I meet his gaze head on, silently confirming I won't be bullied. "So what if he's older? Whatever. And who cares what he does as long as it's a steady job and it pays well? So he's not a lawyer or doctor. Big freaking whoop! In case you've failed to notice, I'm a dentist. I don't need anyone to pay my way." I suppress the scream that's bubbling in my throat, threatening to shatter my bay windows on the way out.

"It's a big deal if you're thinking about getting serious with him. You aren't looking at the big picture, sis."

"Please, enlighten me, brother. What big picture am I missing?" I ask. The sarcasm sticks to my words like molasses.

"Let's say you marry this guy," he says.

"Ramtin," I clarify.

"Let's say you marry *Ramtin*."

I squeeze my fingers together tighter, trying to avoid reaching across the table and slapping him. I roll my shoulders trying to disperse the tension as he continues with his explanation of all the reasons why I shouldn't be with my boyfriend.

"Is he going to want to have kids? You're still young and have plenty of time for babies. Does he want to start all over again with a newborn?" I don't have an answer, so I avert my gaze away from his accusatory glare. "Are you kidding me?" Maziar misses nothing. "Have you even talked about this yet?" he asks, finding a chink in my armor.

"We just started dating. It hasn't been that long. We aren't even thinking about marriage and definitely not babies." I try to enforce my point, pouring as much confidence into my tone as I can. It falls flat, even to my own ears.

"Well, you should!" Maziar's voice rises in frustration.

"Why do you even care?" I yell back, meeting his advancements, octave for octave.

"Because you're my sister! Jeez, Bita. What kind of question is that? I care about you, and I don't want you to make a mistake. Is that so hard to believe?"

"No, it isn't," I admit. "But I'm happy, Maziar. I deserve to be happy."

"Yes, you do. Just with someone else." The finality in his tone makes me cringe.

I stare at my brother, the concern mingled with anger, hovering in his calico hazel eyes. There's a hint of green in them today, reflecting off the olive toned t-shirt he's wearing. I know he's worried and I know that he means well, despite how unwarranted his intrusion is. But, no matter how many points he makes, he won't be able to sway me. I love Ramtin.

I don't know if he wants more children, and I'm aware I need to have this conversation with him, but honestly, if he says he doesn't, I may be okay with it. I have never felt this way before, never knew what it meant to be in love. It feels as though someone has ripped my heart out of my chest and handed it to Ramtin for safekeeping. A part of me will always be his, and right now, that's all I can think about.

"You should go."

Maziar's scowl loosens into wide-eyed shock. He's rendered speechless as I lean back in my chair and hold my ground. After what feels like forever, he finally finds his tongue.

"Are you serious?"

"Yes."

"Bita," he starts, but I raise my hand and stop him midsentence.

"Maziar, I'm not going to end things with Ramtin. It doesn't matter what you say. And the fact that you're sitting here, blatantly making it known that you're totally against my relationship with him, proves that you've learned nothing from your own experience with Sara." I lean forward, my palms spread out on the table, my vision blurred with disappointment. "If going through all of that didn't change you, and you can't see that this is the exact same situation, just with different details, then nothing I say will make a difference. And we don't have anything left to talk about." I stand up. "You can let yourself out." I head to my room, making sure I don't turn back.

I hear Maziar shuffling around the house, certain he's going to barge into my bedroom and demand we talk this out. But he never comes. Ten minutes later, I hear the front door shut, listen to the purring of his engine fire up as he pulls out of my driveway. When I make it out to the kitchen, I find a clean table, his peace offering now thrown uneaten in the trash.

My heart crumbles onto the kitchen tiles, red pain against the stark white of my floors. A sob shudders through me, knowing that I don't have the support of the most important person in my world. Guess this is payback for when I didn't have his back, despite all the amends I've tried to make.

Karma is such a bitch.

* * *

"How was your day?" Ramtin asks. He puts the glass of whiskey against his lips, the edge of the cup seductively caressing his pink flesh. His lashes frame deep pools of chocolate, deliciously nestled in his expression as he watches me closely.

I absentmindedly gnaw on the inside of my cheek, wishing the table were smaller and I could easily make my way over to his lap, wrapping my arms tightly around his neck. I want to get lost in his touch, escape in the way his kiss feels on my skin.

This morning's run-in with my brother has left me agitated and wound up tight. I need a way to shed the tension, find a light at the end of a seemingly desolate tunnel. A night curled up with Ramtin's naked body against mine will do just that.

"It was fine," I answer.

"What did you do?"

I don't answer immediately, debating on whether I should tell him the truth. Do I divulge the details of my brother's disdain for our relationship and ruin the night? What would be the point? There's no sense in upsetting us both. Only one of us needs to have their feelings hurt by Maziar's lack of support.

"I was home. Just did stuff around the house. Cleaned. You know, that sort of thing. Nothing exciting." Not a total lie, but not the whole truth.

"That's cool. It's nice to do nothing sometimes."

"Yeah, it is. Work's been hectic, way too many patients in one day. Staying in sweats was highly needed," I add.

He smiles, the edges of his lips causing lines to fan out from his eyelids. The glow of the industrial lamps adorning the ceiling of the restaurant emphasize Ramtin's wrinkles, soft lines billowing out from his features. Unseen, if not focused on. The gray peppering his hair is oddly stark in this light.

For the first time, I wonder what we look like to the spectators around us. Do they know I'm having dinner with my boyfriend? Are they wondering why I'm here with a guy his age? Or do they think there's a different explanation for our outing? They wouldn't think he was my dad, would they? No, Ramtin looks younger than his age, but nonetheless, the thought makes my stomach roil. I fidget in my seat as

I glance around the room, scoping out the crowd. No one is watching us, too preoccupied with their own dinners to worry about mine.

I shake my head, trying to dislodge the insecurity that curiously has made its way to the forefront of my mind. This is all Maziar's fault. I was fine before he opened his big mouth and placed the seed of doubt. *I need to remember that I don't care what people think.*

Ramtin reaches across the table and places his hand on top of mine. The heat of his fingers courses through my veins, waking me from my moment of uncertainty. The desire in his eyes reminds me of what it is I'm fighting for. It sends chills up my spine.

"I missed you today," he admits.

The heat rises further up my body, wrapping its fingers through my chest, growing with each beat of my heart. "I missed you, too."

We haven't eaten dinner yet. His whiskey and my glass of wine flank a plate of calamari between us. But I'm no longer aware of my hunger. I need to nourish my body, in ways on which food has no effect. I lean forward in my chair, lowering my voice to a hoarse whisper so no one can hear me when I say, "How about we get out of here?"

His lips curl up in a mischievous grin, but I'm cut off by the rude blaring of Ramtin's cell phone. The playful smirk he's wearing falls from his face as he pulls it from his pocket and looks down at the screen. "Sorry," he mumbles, fumbling with the phone. "Hold that thought."

Disappointment drops to my toes, anchoring me heavily in my seat.

"Yasi?" he says. "Everything okay? Wait. What? Slow down. I can't understand you." He raises his finger in a gesture of pause as he stands up and heads toward the entrance of the restaurant.

I watch his sleek back as he makes his way to the door, disappearing into the crowd waiting at the hostess table. I sink even further into my chair.

"Damn it," I mumble to myself, gulping down the remainder of my drink. *My stupid luck.*

This wouldn't be the first time his eldest has found a way to ruin our night. It's as if she has some superpowered radar that signals each time her dad is with me and the exact moment she can do the most damage. I huff at the irritating turn of events and try to get the waitress's attention. When she looks in my direction, I raise my glass and softly wiggle it so she knows it's empty.

By the time Ramtin returns to the table, I'm more than halfway through my new glass of wine and the waitress has come by twice to take our order, only to be shooed away when she sees my date is still missing.

"I have to go," Ramtin announces, abruptly. He collects his keys off the table and shoves them into his coat pocket, pulling out his wallet instead.

"What?" There's no hiding how annoyed I am, evident in the harsh tone of my voice.

He looks at me with a puzzled expression plastered on his face. Then, suddenly realizing that hastily cutting our date short without explanation is impolite, his expression softens when he adds, "Yasi and her mom got into a big fight. She's really upset and crying. I need to go pick her up."

I want to say that she's a kid and kids don't always get along with their parents, that coming in for the rescue and whisking her away from a situation she isn't happy with isn't doing her any favors. But then, what kind of woman would I be if I wanted him to choose me over his own children? Yes, I want to be the center of his universe, but do I really want a guy who cares more about the woman he's dating than about his kids? A conundrum, to want to be someone's world but know, if you are, that makes him a selfish person.

"Okay." I know anything more would show one of us in an unflattering light. "I can get the tab."

"Don't be silly." He raises his hand and gestures to the waitress to bring us our check. "I'll take you home before I head over to Roya's."

"I'm going to go to the bathroom, then, while we wait on the bill."

Once inside the ladies' room, I find a stall. I rest my head against the cool metal door and take a few deep breaths to calm my nerves. *This is totally fine. His daughter is having a rough day; that's all. She's not trying to ruin our night.* I try to convince myself that there's nothing to be jealous of.

But the sad truth is that I am jealous.

Later that evening, as I lay in bed, staring at the flashing images across my television screen, I wonder if I'll always play second fiddle in Ramtin's world. I don't want to admit that Maziar has a point, but he does. Maybe not directly, but there's something to be said that the man I love has an entire other life he's lived without me. One I can't compare to, with kids and memories I'll never be a part of.

Would he want to start all over? With me this time? And if he does, will he love our baby as much as he loves his girls? Or will they always have a deeper place in his heart because they came first?

And let's not get started on Yasi. Kimiya is less of a worry, her sweet demeanor leading me to believe that I could forge a relationship with her and that she may get a little excited if there ever were a baby sibling. But Yasi, that girl is the devil in disguise, all sweet and sticky with her "Daddy, I love you," and "I'm the luckiest girl," but secretly plotting to tear him away from me.

Ugh, Bita, stop it. She's just a kid. I'm almost embarrassed by the thoughts running through my mind, but then I reach over and feel the empty space beside me on the bed. The sheets are still cool and unwrinkled by the lack of Ramtin's body, his absence stark against the darkness of the bedroom. I sigh, my mind racing in directions I'm not comfortable with, a knot now lodged in my throat.

I'm so lost in the battle raging on inside me that I'm dramatically startled by the ringing of my phone as I nearly fall off the bed. Shaking my head and laughing at myself, I reach over to grab it off the nightstand.

"Hello," I answer.

"Hi, *eshgham. My love.*" Ramtin's voice floods my insides with relief. "What are you doing?"

"Nothing. I'm lying in bed, channel surfing," I say. "What are you doing?"

"The same."

"How's Yasi?" I have to force the words through my lips as if they're shards of glass I'm trying to avoid. *This is ridiculous. What is wrong with me?*

"She's fine. She's asleep now."

"Did she tell you what happened?" *That was so important she had to mess up our night?*

"Yeah. Just a mother-daughter argument. You know how they go. She was just being dramatic." I roll my eyes. I could have guessed that, but I don't point it out. "I'm sorry about tonight," he apologizes, prompting the lump to resurface. "I really wanted to spend it with you."

"Me too."

He has no idea how much I needed him tonight. But then again, how could he? I didn't tell him the truth about my day. He has no idea that my heart is broken over my brother's opinion about our relationship. I can't hold what he doesn't know against him.

"Okay, *eshgham*." His term of endearment cuts like a knife in the solitude of my room. "I just wanted to check in before I went to bed. Sleep well, okay? I'll see you tomorrow."

"Yeah. See you tomorrow. Goodnight."

"*Shab bekhehr. Goodnight.* I love you."

My heart constricts, wondering if love is enough to get us through the plethora of obstacles that have presented themselves. Will it act as a weapon aiding in our success, or will it just be collateral damage after the war is lost?

"I love you, too."

CHAPTER EIGHT

I pace the living room, my nerves having me bent up in knots. I shake my fingers out, trying to expel the anxious energy through their tips. It doesn't work so I resort to flapping my arms up and down like a bird, trying to keep the inevitable sweat rings from making their appearance on my shirt. Ramtin is on his way over to pick me up. With his daughters.

I know I shouldn't be this wound up over it, but I can't help that I am. The attitude I'll get from Yasi, along with the monumental meltdown she most definitely will have, is making me dread this outing before it's even begun.

I was apprehensive when Ramtin suggested we hang out with his girls. It's been five months since we started dating, and it's obvious things have gotten serious between us. The families, though, have been kept at bay for the most part, neither of us wanting to ruin the honeymoon phase of our relationship. I want to indulge in the tender moments of the beginning before we have the house come crashing down on us. Ramtin, being the more mature one it seems, is taking the first plunge into these dangerous waters. Which, in turn, means I will have to as well, and the rubble will sadly find its way to bury us.

The doorbell rings, jarring me from my thoughts. I take a sharp breath, rub my sweaty palms across my jeans, and swing the door open. He stands a few feet in front of me, navy blue t-shirt accentuating his dark features, smile stretched across his face. My gaze instinctively finds the small scar beneath his left eye, a sign of familiarity that gives me comfort in the chaos of my mind.

"Hey, *eshgham*," he says, leaning in and kissing me softly. "Are you ready?"

I make the rookie mistake of glancing over his shoulder toward the car where a very unhappy Yasi is staring at me sideways, hands crossed defiantly over her chest. I exhale. *This is going to be a rough morning.*

"Yeah, I'm ready," I answer, even though I'm not.

He holds my hand as he walks me over to the passenger side, opening the door for me as usual, then softly kissing the top of my hand before helping me in. All the while, Yasi tracks us like a hunter getting ready to attack her prey. I have to consciously tell myself not to throw my bag at her. That would definitely end badly. So instead, I plaster on my best happy face as I turn toward the back seat.

"Hey, girls." My voice is too chipper. It's annoying, even to me. "How are you guys?"

Kimiya smiles innocently.

"We're fine," Yasi answers in a clipped tone, cutting off any response her younger sister may have had. Kimiya winces, Yasi's rude behavior too blatant to ignore. She gives me a regretful nod before staring out her window.

"Well, that's good." I turn to face the front of the car and pretend I don't notice Yasi's bitchiness.

Ramtin has made his way back over to the driver's seat. "I'm so excited that I get to spend the day with all three of my girls," he says as he reverses down the driveway.

I can't help but smirk. Despite not turning around, I imagine Yasi's crimson face, livid that somehow I've become one of her dad's "girls." Childish, I know, but I'm going to give myself this little win.

Thirty minutes later, we're pulling into the miniature golf parking lot. Yasi huffs as she unfolds her lanky frame from the car, and Kimiya bounces on the balls of her feat, the only one excited for today's endeavor. Her, and possibly Ramtin. I can't tell if he really thinks this will be a fantastic day, or if he's just faking it for the sake of maintaining peace.

Kimiya comes up beside him and wraps her fingers around his. He leans down and kisses her head. Yasi quickly makes it over to his other side, nestling beneath the crook of his arm, safely wrapped in her father's cocoon. *Well played, little princess, well played.* With nowhere else to go, I step up beside Kimiya. Ramtin gives me an apologetic smile over her head and winks.

He buys our tickets and we select our clubs and color-coordinate our balls, heading out to the first hole on the green. It's a big white castle with a blue, tiled roof.

"I'm going first," Yasi demands. She looks at me and waits.

I don't know if she's expecting me to react, scream and stamp my foot that I should go first. Does she realize I'm not a child? Or is her perception of my age skewed? I nod and point my chin in the direction of the castle, urging her to take her turn. She smirks and hits the ball.

For the next hour, I watch Ramtin guide his girls through each hole, clapping when they make it and letting them have a redo when they don't. I stand back, quietly observing, trying to remind myself that losing their father to another woman, who isn't their mother, is hard for teenagers. I do my best to ask the right questions and prompt the girls to engage in conversation with me. By the time we make it to the eighteenth hole, Kimiya is chatting up a storm. She's told me about her friends and what it's like to be in middle school. I've learned that English is her favorite subject and that she loves to read. She's shared that her dream is to be a novelist someday. I forget about the daggers Yasi stares in my direction and let myself enjoy her little sister's company.

When we head back to the car to go to lunch, Kimiya reaches out and holds my hand as we debate between French fries or Chinese food. I can feel the tension draining from my shoulders and the hope blooming in my chest. Maybe this could work. I almost forget about the fury lurking in the shadows, the unamused daughter with plans of her own.

French fries win as Ramtin heads toward the nearest In-and-Out.

I'm so content in the current state I'm in that I lose myself in the conversation, and when Ramtin reaches out and holds my hand, lifting it to his lips, I hear myself say, "I love you," before I know what I'm doing.

Silence falls across the car, the tapping of Yasi's foot the only thing that can be heard. It's like the rumble of a train, low and slow but picking up speed the closer it gets. It all happens so quickly from here that if feels like a flash of light. The clouds move in, the lighting strikes, as the roar of thunder bursts through the she-devil.

"You've got to be fucking kidding me!" Yasi yells.

"Yasi!" Ramtin's voice booms against the walls of the car.

Yasi doesn't even blink at his reprimand as she moves forward in her seat, her icy glare pinning me to mine. "You love him?" she growls. "Well, too bad. He already has a family that loves him, and you aren't in it!"

My throat goes dry and I lose my words. My own fury is strangling me, but I know I can't react to her outburst. I shouldn't have gotten swept up in the moment and let down my guard. I shouldn't have let my emotions muddle my better senses. Why would I say that? Why would I tell Ramtin I loved him in front of his daughters? What's wrong with me?

Despite the desire to revert to my seventeen-year-old self and engage in this battle of wills with Yasi, it wouldn't get us anywhere. And I need for this to work, regardless of how dim the outcome looks now. Or how much I can't stand her. Plus, Ramtin has already pulled over and turned in his seat, meeting his teenage daughter with an even more impressive glare.

"You apologize to Bita right now," he demands.

"For what? Telling her the truth? Look at her," she says, waving her hand in my direction. "She looks like she could be in my geometry class!"

She's lost complete control, her face flushed with anger, her nostrils flaring with each inhale, her leg tapping so hard against the floor of the car, I'm afraid she'll break though like Rumpelstiltskin.

"Yasi, calm down!" Ramtin yells.

I'm afraid she may start hyperventilating.

"Yasi, I'm sorry for saying that in front of you guys. It was inappropriate," I apologize, in an attempt to calm the situation.

Ramtin reaches out and grabs my hand. I almost pull it away. Any physical contact will just make this already horrendous situation worse.

"You did nothing wrong," Ramtin insists, then turns toward his daughters. "I love Bita and she loves me. I'm sorry that isn't easy for you to accept." His tone softens as the tears start streaming down Yasi's face. My chest begins to ache. I didn't want to break her heart, but somehow, it seems like I have. "I will always love you guys, and nothing and no one will change that. I need you to believe me."

"What about Mom?" Kimiya asks. Until now, I've forgotten she's in the car. She's been sitting quiet as a mouse, hidden in the corner of the seat. Now she stares at her father, wide-eyed and terrified.

"I'll always love your mother, too. Because she gave me the best gift ever — the two of you. You're the most important people to me. And I wouldn't have you without your mom. But I don't love her the way you guys may want me to. You know this; we've talked about it. I'm really sorry if that hurts you. I never want to hurt you guys." The pain in his voice is audible as he struggles to push the words out of his lungs. My heart constricts further.

Kimiya doesn't cry. She looks between her father, the woman he's now in love with, and her sobbing sister, and her expression falls into oblivion. She's too young to appear this exhausted, but something tells me this family feud has been going on longer than just in this car.

Her sad eyes find mine and she tries her best to smile. The corners of her lips can only manage a twitch. Then she reaches out and grabs Yasi's hand, returning her gaze to the window, staring at the cars driving by.

"Why can't you just leave us alone?" Yasi barks, half mumble, half sob.

"Yasi," Ramtin responds. He's not yelling, but there's no mistaking his anger. Before I have a chance to say anything, he adds, "I'm taking you guys home."

"Whatever," Yasi replies, throwing me one last dirty look before turning her head toward the window. She doesn't have to admit it, but I know she hates me.

I inhale, wanting to find the right words to turn this all around. I wish there was something I could say to make me less of a threat and more of a friend. But I know that short of leaving their father's life, there isn't much I can do to rectify the situation. Not now, anyway.

Disappointed and deflated, I turn around and stare out onto the street, praying this ride of doom is over soon.

* * *

Ramtin insisted on staying the night. Now he lies beside me, his arm draped over my stomach, nuzzled in close to my shoulder. He breathes heavily with sleep, and I'm envious because I can't close my eyes. There are too many hurdles in the way of dreams.

What am I going to do about Ramtin's daughters? And what the hell am I going to do about my family? Those are two wars I've been trying to avoid. But despite being drained from the most recent ordeal, I know I can't delay it much longer.

Maziar has kept his mouth shut out of sibling courtesy, but he won't keep it to himself for very long. And at this point, isn't it better to see where we stand in this shitstorm instead of hiding behind some façade of a Happily Ever After? That doesn't seem like the probable outcome anymore. We'll be lucky if there's a happily anything in our future.

Somewhere between three and four in the morning, as I hash out battle plans, I doze off. I'm startled awake at seven when my doorbell rings nonstop.

"What the hell?" Ramtin mumbles, his voice hoarse and groggy.

I blink a few times trying to clear away the heavy blanket of sleep. I'm so tired that I'm not entirely sure I'm awake and this isn't a dream. But the bell doesn't stop.

"Who's here this early on a Sunday?"

"I don't know. I'm not expecting anyone," I answer, swinging my legs over the side of the bed. "I'll go see."

Ramtin is stretching and unfolding himself out from beneath the covers, when I wrap a robe around my shoulders and head to the front of the house. I don't even bother to look through the window, too drowsy to care who's standing there. I just want to go back to bed. I open the door, mid-yawn, to find Roya waiting impatiently on my porch.

Her hands are on her hips, her foot tapping furiously on the floor, and her face is in a scowl. Eyebrows pinched in tight, lips drawn down in a frown.

"Roya?" *Why is my boyfriend's ex-wife at my house?*

"Where's Ramtin? I need to talk to him," she demands, standing on her tiptoes to look behind me. She huffs when she doesn't see him. "Is he here?"

I exhale. Breathing seems like the only thing left to do, now that the drama has officially made its way to my doorstep.

"Yeah. Come in." I move aside and let her pass.

"Roya?" Ramtin stands frozen between the hallway and the living room, as thrown off to see his ex as I am. "What are you doing here?"

"We need to talk," she insists. Then looks in my direction. "Alone."

Ramtin's face balls up in anger and I can see the red creeping up the skin of his neck. I step in, trying to diffuse the potential bomb.

"Why don't you guys hang in the living room while I make us some *chayee?*" I offer. "It's early, and we could all use the caffeine."

Roya finds her manners. *"Merci, Bita joon. Thank you, dear Bita.* That would be great," she says, then gives me a dismissive courtesy smile.

I grab Ramtin's arm on my way to the kitchen and squeeze with reassurance. I want him to know that she's not offending me. He leans in and kisses my cheek, then heads to the couch to deal with Roya. I can hear her huff at his display of affection, but I don't turn around. I gladly welcome the escape, the tension so thick, it fills the room like smoke.

I set the kettle on the stove and lean on the island waiting for the water to boil. I stare out the bay windows watching the leaves blowing in the breeze and the neighbors going about their business. I try to absorb the serenity of the scene, allowing its energy to wrap me up like a warm throw blanket. I know it'll last but only a moment.

As if on cue, Roya and Ramtin begin to yell. I pinch the bridge of my nose, trying to squeeze away the headache that's now nestled between my eyes. I don't mean to eavesdrop, but they're so loud I can't help it.

"*Ramtin, chekar meekoni bah een dokhtar? What are you doing with this girl?*"

This girl. Apparently, I don't have an identity.

"What do you mean, what am I doing? It's none of your business what I do with anyone," Ramtin answers.

"Yes, it is! We have kids, and when you bring someone around, it is my business. Please tell me you don't see a future here. *Bahchas! She's a child!*"

I drop my head into my hands and groan. When the hell did twenty-eight become a kid? Why is everyone acting like I'm still in high school and Ramtin's some old man?

"*Bahcheh neest. She's not a child.*" At least someone realizes that.

"It's not good for Yasi to see you prancing around with her. She's impressionable. How do you think it makes her feel when her father is playing house with someone who looks more her age than his? *Khejalat Behkesh! Be ashamed of yourself.*"

The kettle begins to whistle, making it difficult to hear what they're saying. I let the sound fill the kitchen, wanting to drown out their conversation. I can't take any more of this nonsense. It's been an uphill battle, and it doesn't appear to be ending any time soon.

I take my time pouring out three glasses of tea before heading back to the living room, where I find a very annoyed Roya glaring at Ramtin, and an even more furious Ramtin, staring back at her. They turn toward me when they hear my feet shuffling across the wood floor.

I place the tray of tea and *shirinee, pastries,* on the coffee table. I saunter past Ramtin with a dramatic sway in my hips, reminding him just how much he wants this "young girl." Still draped in a robe, I take a seat beside him on the couch and do my best to appear confident as I cross my legs and lean forward to grab a cup of tea.

Roya is a force to be reckoned with, taking only a moment to find her bearings before she matches my determination. Ramtin just dumbly looks between the two women in his life, one holding his past and the other hanging onto his future.

"How's Yasi feeling? I hope she's doing better." My sickly-sweet tone drips with fake concern.

"Oh, you know, sometimes change can be tough on a teenager. Seeing her father with someone much younger than himself is hard for her."

"Hmmm. I'm sorry she's having a rough time with it. But this is a great opportunity for Yasi to see how relationships of all shapes and sizes can work out. If we love each other, the rest shouldn't matter."

"Well," Roya starts, but I stand up, stopping her mid-sentence.

"What do I know? I'm just some young girl without kids," I admit, shrugging. "Thanks for stopping by this early on a Sunday morning to drag us out of bed. Maybe next time you guys can meet at a coffee shop and duke this out like normal divorced couples." I put my hand on Ramtin's shoulder. He stares at me, one part irritation, two parts bewilderment. "I'm going to go take a shower. You'll walk Roya out, right, my love?" I don't wait for a response, just sashay down the hall to my bedroom.

Once inside, the anger I've kept locked up bubbles to the surface in the form of slamming drawers and throwing pillows across the room. Realizing I need a more productive way to expel my hostile energy, I go about tidying up. My bed is made with military precision as I yank hard on the sheets and press down to make the creases. Just as I'm returning the last pillow to its rightful location, the door swings open.

"What the hell was that?" Ramtin asks.

Despite his lean frame, he fills the doorway with his towering rage. This only provokes my own anger as I puff up my chest in response. I refuse to be on the receiving end of anyone's disappointment right now, least of all the boyfriend whose ex-wife just barged rudely into my home to let me know I'm not good enough to be in his life.

I turn, focused intently on my target. "Excuse me?" My voice is eerily calm despite the storm raging inside me.

"What was that?" he repeats.

"I heard you the first time. I'm not hard of hearing," I clarify. "I'm just not sure what you're referring to." I force the words through gritted teeth.

"Let me elaborate," he says, taking a step closer. "Why would you feel the need to throw yourself into the conversation? It was already heated enough as it was."

"Are you kidding me? Was I supposed to just sit back and let your ex talk shit about me in my own home? She's the one who felt she had the right to come barging into my place to seek you out for a conversation that could have waited."

"Yasi was really upset last night. That's why she wanted to deal with it first thing."

"Oh, please!" I hiss. "If you believe that, then you're the naïve child. She showed up here to stake some sort of nonexistent dominance. She wanted to fluff her feathers around my territory to show me who's boss. Up until this moment, I would have been certain she had no claims to you, but by the way you're trying to defend her right now, I may be wrong." I glare at him, my fingers twitching by my sides, wanting nothing more than to pummel him for his stupidity.

"I'm not defending her. I'm just saying that when it comes to my kids, maybe you should stay out of it and let the parents figure it out."

"Then figure it out somewhere else!" I shout. I quickly lose control over my emotions, anger and disappointment filling my soul like the demons they are.

"Now you're acting like a child. And here I thought Yasi was the dramatic one." He shakes his head.

"Don't even get me started on her!" *Why did I just say that?*

Classic Bita move. Why do I always speak before thinking, react before I've had a chance to hash it out in my mind? Maziar would say I'm volatile and irrational. The rush of anger I'm feeling transforms into a storm, drowning me.

"What is that supposed to mean?" His nostrils flare, and he's panting with fury.

"Screw you, Ramtin," I reply. *Nice, Bita.*

"You know what? I think I should leave." He is seething.

"Fabulous idea."

He walks over to the chair and collects his clothes. He's already in a pair of sweats, pulling his t-shirt over his head without a second glance.

"We'll speak later," he calls over his shoulder, as he heads down the hall.

I hear the front door thud into place, the sound an echoing discontent in my head. I grab the pillow I've just placed back on the bed and throw it across the room, as I scream for no one to hear.

CHAPTER NINE

"Doctor Hakimi," Haley says, pulling my attention away from the patient in my chair.

I look over my shoulder, irritation for the interruption flashing as a warning in my glare. She hesitates, then gives me an apologetic smile. I turn back to my patient.

"I'm so sorry. Could you excuse me for just a moment?"

"Sure," he answers.

I walk over to where Haley is now standing in the hallway.

"What is it?" My tone is clipped, causing her to flinch.

"There's someone here to see you."

"Who is it?"

"Ramtin."

"What is he doing here?" I ask, knowing Haley has no clue. Nonetheless, she stares at me dumbfounded, unsure how she should answer that question. "Did he tell you what he wanted?"

"Not specifically. He just asked if I could let you know he was here."

I exhale, deep and slow. It's been two days since the blowout at my house. We haven't talked much. He's attempted to call but I haven't reciprocated his efforts.

I'm in uncharted territory and need a minute to gather my thoughts. There's so many things I want to say to Ramtin, so many aspects of that morning that pissed me off, but I know it wouldn't help. Because I can't trust myself not to be impulsive, or trust that I can keep Crazy Bita at bay, I've resorted to avoiding him until I can cool off. Apparently, Ramtin doesn't appreciate my attempt at maturity.

"Tell him I'm with a patient and it will be a little while," I direct.

"Okay," Haley answers. "Should I have him wait in your office?"

"Yeah, sure."

I return to my patient and finish the exam. I'm on autopilot as I explain the technicalities of a root canal and why he'll need a crown afterwards. I answer his numerous questions with accuracy, all the while my mind wandering to the man a few feet away from me, waiting in my office.

I'm still unsure of how much of my feelings I should disclose, afraid that another argument, in the workplace no less, could potentially end badly on various levels. My boss would be pissed if we're yelling, and the rumor mill will have a field day with it. I'm already known as the "bitchy, demanding doctor." Wouldn't they love to know that it's not all roses and butterflies in my life? How satisfying that would be for some of them.

"If you follow me up to the front desk, Mr. Land, I'll have the girls schedule your next appointment and go over all the insurance details with you."

I smile as I stand aside, allowing him to walk out into the hall before me. Once I've successfully handed him off, I turn on my heels and make my way over to my office. I take a minute, hand resting on the doorknob, to gather my thoughts and reel in my nerves, before going inside.

I find Ramtin standing beside the small bookshelf lining the back wall of my little space. He's staring at the two picture frames sitting there, one of my parents, one of Maziar and Sara. I've thought about putting up a photo of us but am suddenly relieved I've procrastinated, unsure if it would appear premature to a man Ramtin's age. We've only been dating for a few months, and I'm lost in the arena of relationship etiquette. Is it immature to make the effort to frame a memory after such a short period of time, even if I'm in love with him? My lack of experience in love, in addition to the added layer of dating an older man, leaves me clueless and questioning myself most days.

Despite my hating to admit it, the entire run-in with Roya has made me incredibly insecure about my age. I never viewed myself as exceptionally young, but in comparison to the forty-somethings, maybe I'm just being naïve. And the fact that my significant other lives this double life of boyfriend one day, ex-husband and father the next, isn't helping either.

Ramtin turns when he hears me shut the door. He doesn't say anything at first, his gaze slowly running along the features of my face, sweeping across my eyes, my nose, and settling on my lips. It lingers heavily on my flesh, causing goosebumps to rise across my skin. I can almost feel his lips grazing mine, even though he's standing a few feet away. An ache starts deep inside me with the alarming realization of how much my body craves his touch.

"Hi," he says, his voice a hoarse whisper.

"Hi."

"You haven't been taking my calls." Apparently, we're getting straight to the point.

I break the staring contest, making my way over to the desk and sitting down. He follows suit, taking one of the two seats placed across from me. I'm hoping this big block of wood separating us will allow me to stay focused. His proximity has a way of making me dizzy, causing me to forget why I'm even upset.

"I needed time to think."

"About?"

"About the other morning. About what we're doing here. About all of it."

He leans back, resting his elbows on the armrest of the chair, clasping his hands in front of him. His head is slightly cocked to one side in thought. I know he's analyzing me, and it makes me uncomfortable. I have to force myself not to fidget.

Ramtin has an uncanny way of peering into my soul and seeing the things I try to keep hidden, even from myself. He reads me like a story he's heard so many times it's now memorized.

I don't want him to discover that I'm no longer sure of his feelings for me or where I stand in the grand scheme of his life. I feel exposed and vulnerable, two emotions I'm uncomfortable with. I hate the instability and the unknown of being in love. I'm used to holding the cards in my hand, having control over my relationships. But somewhere along the line, I've lost my grip, handing my heart over to this man without keeping much of it for myself. And because I have, he now could ruin me. And I hate it.

What if he decides I'm too young, or too immature, or just some hot, young lay? What do I do then? I've been building this dream in my head since I met Ramtin, imagining a future I hadn't realized how badly I wanted.

Calm down, Bita. It's just one fight. I know I'm overreacting. Couples disagree often, so why am I so shaken up? The truth is that it's because our obstacles are greater than the average problems. There's an ex-wife and a horrid teenager and a family I have yet to tell about us. They feel monumental on the relationship food chain.

"And what conclusions have you come up with?" Ramtin asks, breaking me from my internal struggle.

"Honestly, I don't know."

"Okay, how about we try talking about it before we go all 'end of the world' with this?"

"Don't be condescending, Ramtin," I snap, a surge of anger rushing through me. "I'm not one of your daughters."

He pauses, regarding me carefully. I want to retract my words as soon as they leave my lips, feeling childish and bitter.

"I never said you were," Ramtin urges. "I know you aren't my daughters. But since you brought them up, how about we start there?"

"What's there to say?" I want to change the subject. Discussing Yasi will only cause us to combust in my office, a scattered mess of shrapnel and body parts.

"I have a feeling you have a lot to say. More specifically, about Yasi." He leans forward in his chair, moving his elbows to rest on his knees.

"Now is the time to get what you need off your chest, Bita." The ball is in my court and he waits patiently for me to make my move.

I so desperately want to unleash the fury I have eating my insides, tell him how much of a brat he's raised and how someone needs to show that girl real consequences for her actions and rude behavior, but I know it's unacceptable to voice that opinion. I'm just his girlfriend, and that's his flesh and blood. After all, what do I really know about raising children anyway? But at the same time, I don't want to act like how Yasi treats me is acceptable. If nothing else, she should have the common courtesy to keep her blatant disregard for me, to herself. That's just manners.

"Look, I know things got out of hand the other day. I'm truly sorry for admitting I loved you in front of your girls. That was unacceptable."

"It wasn't the best timing, but you didn't do anything wrong, Bita." A small tug appears at the side of his lip, pulling it halfway into a smile. My heart picks up its pace.

"Okay. Then it was bad timing on my part. And I'm really sorry about that." I take a deep breath and clasp my hands on the desk. I try to steady my nerves, taking my time to speak so I don't say something I'll regret. I know I'm treading in dangerous waters. "But the way Yasi talks to me—it's not right, Ramtin. I know she's having a tough time, and I can respect that. But that still doesn't give her a right to be rude." I almost say bitch, relieved I caught myself. That would not bode well for the cause.

"You're absolutely right," he concedes. "Her behavior is definitely inappropriate. Regardless of how she feels, she needs to be kind and respectful. I didn't raise her to be this way, I can assure you." He scoots toward the edge of his chair and reaches out, placing his hand on top of mine. As his palm grazes my skin and the heat seeps into my fingers, my insides begin to melt. I have zero defenses against this man. "I'm going to talk to her. It won't happen again."

I was expecting some opposition, a rebuttal prepared and ready. His cooperation surprises me and encourages me forward.

"And the other morning with Roya? What about that?"

"She shouldn't have shown up at your house like that."

"No, she shouldn't have," I agree. "But she did. She must think she can trample over whomever you date. Otherwise, I can't imagine why she thought that was okay."

"I don't know what she thinks," he admits.

"She thinks she can get away with whatever she wants," I continue. The frustration thickly coating my words. I have to remind myself to hold it together, so I soften my tone when I add, "I'm sorry. I know you're stuck in a tough position, between us all. But Ramtin, I can't deal with Yasi and Roya and my brother. It's all too much."

"Your brother?"

Oh, shit! "Yeah, my brother," I say, averting my gaze to the floor.

"What's going on with your brother?"

"The same as with everyone else," I huff. "Apparently, a fifteen-year age difference is the kiss of death for a relationship. I honestly don't get what all the fuss is about. What difference does it make!" I feel the heat creeping up my cheeks.

"I don't think it makes any difference." He squeezes my hand, his smile finally reaching the edges of his eyes. I love the fragile lines that fan out across his skin. "Look, I get that everyone has their own opinions about us. But that's only their opinion, just as long as we know this is what we want. But if you are doubting that already, then this isn't going to work."

My fear is a loud bitch screaming in my head for me to hightail it out of here. It's only been a few months, so the heartbreak will heal, or at least that's what I'm telling myself. When I think of Roya and Yasi, my insides twist in knots at the potential of having to deal with them forever. I don't know if I have it in me to put up with their ridiculous antics without losing my shit. But at the same time, as Ramtin stares at me with those soft, deep eyes, I know I can't walk away. I'm too selfish to give up what I have, even for the part of me that's petrified of what this will do to me if I lose him in the end.

"Do you want this, Bita?"

"Yes," I hear myself whisper.

"Good." He makes his way over to my side of the desk and pulls me up from my seat. He leans close to my ear, his breath hot on my skin when he says, "Because I love you." He kisses the crook of my neck and I'm instantly lightheaded. "So much," he adds, his lips grazing the edge of my jaw. "More than you could imagine." He catches my lower lip between his teeth, and I fear I'll lose my footing and pass out. He wraps his arms around my waist and pulls me into his chest. I can feel his heart beating against my breasts, the rhythmic thump picking up pace as his lips come crashing into mine.

I love you so much it terrifies me.

I melt into him, my fingers tangled in his hair as I press my body to meet his. My pulse quickens, and my need for him burns through my limbs. He kisses me deeply, and I want to tear his clothes off and take him on my office floor. My hands selfishly find the edge of his shirt, smuggling their way beneath the fabric. I run my fingers across his hot, sweaty skin, wishing my lips could follow in their footsteps. We get lost in the moment, unaware of our surroundings until a knock at the door rudely interrupts us. When he pulls away, he leaves me breathless and wanting.

"Doctor, you have rooms two and three ready," my assistant informs me.

"Okay, I'll be right there." I look up at Ramtin. "Why won't they leave me alone?"

He laughs. "We'll pick this up later tonight?"

"Definitely."

"Good." He gently kisses the tip of my nose, then my lips. "Till then, *eshgham*." He winks and heads out my office door.

I watch Ramtin's lean, muscular frame as it disappears down the hallway, taking my doubts and concerns along with him.

* * *

The scents of turmeric and onion hit my nose as I step through the door. I drop my bag on the couch and throw my jacket over the arm rest, making my way into the kitchen. I stand in the doorway, leaning against the frame, taking in the spectacular view.

Ramtin is in front of the stove, stirring what appears to be *khoresht, stew*, as a pot of water boils beside him. I can see the grains of rice popping up to the surface, even from this distance. The sign the rice is ready to be strained and steamed to perfection, so he can make *tadig*, *crispy rice*. An Iranian favorite, almost universally.

He doesn't notice I'm here, his phone playing Dave Matthews as he sings under his breath along with it. I watch the muscles flex beneath his shirt with each move he makes, lost in the task at hand. There's nothing quite as sexy as a Persian man cooking. It's not as common as one would think, especially a man from his generation. I'm suddenly so happy I decided to give him a key.

He turns toward the fridge to grab something, when he spots me.

"Oh, hey," he says, grinning. "I didn't hear you."

"I know."

"Have you been standing there long?"

"Nope, just a minute. You were so focused I didn't want to interrupt you." I walk over to

the stove. "What are you making?"

"*Khoreshteh Ghemeh. Split pea stew.* Are you hungry?"

"I'm starving," I admit, lifting the lid to peer inside. The red-orange stew bubbles and my

stomach growls with approval.

He wraps his arms around my waist. "Why don't you go shower? It'll be ready when

you're done." He kisses the crown of my head.

I turn in his embrace and wrap my arms around his neck, pressing my lips to his. He

tastes of tomato sauce and familiarity. When he chuckles, he makes my soul feel alive.

"You're going to make me burn the food," he teases. "Go take your shower."

"Okay, okay." I playfully raise my hands in defeat. "You're no fun."

"I'm no fun?" He pulls me into him again and nibbles on my ear. "I'll show you just how fun I am after dinner." He winks, then smacks my ass as I strut my way out of the kitchen, making me giddy with content.

Ten minutes later, I'm standing in the bathroom with a towel wrapped around my chest, wet hair splayed across my shoulders. I stare at myself in the mirror, my green eyes bright against my olive skin. I put on a red lace bra and the matching panties and am about to throw on my sweats but stop as I catch a glimpse of my body in the full-length mirror. The curve of my hips and the swell of my breasts complement the lingerie, giving me courage. I leave the sweats on my chair as I make my way out of the bedroom.

I find Ramtin still in the kitchen, plating dinner and setting the table. Dave Matthews continues to play in the background as he hums along with it. He puts two dishes down and turns to find me standing a few feet away from him, leaning against the wall. He stops and stares, taking in the contours of my outfit, or lack thereof, just as I'd hoped.

"How hungry are you?" I ask, tilting my head and smirking.

"Not that hungry," he answers, taking three big strides to close the distance between us.

Before I know it, his arms are wrapped around me and he's kissing me hard, his tongue finding mine as it dances to our own personal melody. I frantically fumble with his zipper, getting it undone and pushing his pants to the floor. My hand wraps around his hard flesh and he gasps with pleasure. Satisfaction flaps in my chest at his response to my touch.

The bay window gives my neighborhood a perfect view of our indecent exposure, but I don't care, so lost in the feel of Ramtin's hands across my skin, his mouth on mine, his need pulsating against my fingers. He creates a trail of kisses down my neck as I pull his shirt up over his head. I drop it onto the floor and have to catch my breath as I peer at his naked body. He's etched to perfection like a Greek god.

I tangle my fingers through his hair, standing on tiptoes to reach his mouth. He lifts me up as I wrap my legs around his waist and carries me over to the couch. His lips find my breast, his tongue teasing my nipple through the thin fabric.

"I want you so bad," I whisper against his ear, and he groans, pulling my nipple between his teeth.

He gently places me down on the couch and unlatches my bra in one swift motion. He doesn't wait for me to take off my panties, just pulls the lace aside and enters me. His erection is hard with his need for me, each thrust building with intensity until I swear I can't take any more. His mouth leaves an expert trail of lips and tongue across my body, finding all the tender places that make me ache and moan.

The moment builds, the need swells, and the orgasm explodes between us, so big it feels like the house is shaking. I scream out his name as we both find the sweet release of lovemaking. Panting and blissfully exhausted, Ramtin's body collapses on top of mine as he lays soft kisses along my collar bone. Naked and content, I run my fingers lazily down his back, creating swirling patterns.

"Maybe we should fight more often," Ramtin suggests, lifting himself up so I can see his smirk.

"And why is that?" I tease.

"Because I always want to have make-up sex with you." He dips his head down and lays a kiss in the triangle created at the base of my neck. Goosebumps fan out across my flesh.

"How about we just have make-up sex, minus the fights?"

"Yeah, we can do that." He moves back up, catching my bottom lip between his teeth in a seductive nibble. "You starving yet?" he asks, making his way back down to my breast.

"Not yet," I answer, breathless. Food is the furthest thing from my mind.

"Good." He presses me down into the couch cushions, as he takes me again.

CHAPTER TEN

"**M**om?" I call, when I find the living room empty.

"I'm in here." Her voice floats in from the kitchen.

As I make my way down the hall, I can hear her singing. Googoosh is playing in the background, the melody filling the room with some famous depressing ballad. I stand in the doorway watching her mess with the dials of her Persian radio, trying to decrease the background static. She loves that dinky thing, a definitive blast from the past, resembling a mini-boom box. I've tried to get her a more modern one, but she refuses, too attached to her dated model.

She doesn't notice as I stand a few feet behind her, enjoying the little concert. Some of my earliest memories of Mom are when she'd sing to my brother and me. If she hadn't moved to the States with Dad, I bet she could have been a famous Iranian singer.

Her voice elicits the comfort of the past, filling my insides like warm coals from a fire. I get lost in her song, forgetting I'm no longer my five-year-old self.

"*Tooyeh yek deevareh sangy, dotah panjereh hast. Dotah khasteh, dotah tanhah, yekeehshoon toh, yekeeshoon man,*" she sings. *In a brick wall there are two windows. Both tired and both alone. One of them is you and one of them is me.*

I smile when I realize she's singing my favorite Googoosh song.

She turns to grab lettuce off the kitchen counter, while humming and swaying to the music, when she spots me.

"Oh!" She laughs. "How long have you been standing there watching me make a fool of myself?"

"Not long. And I love the way you sing." I make my way over to her and kiss the crown of her graying head.

She wraps her arms around me and squeezes tight. The smell of her perfume, mixed with the scent of her skin, reminds me of home.

"I've missed you, *azizam*."

"I've missed you too, Mom." I love having my privacy, but some nights after a long day at work, I do wish Mom was there to have *cheyee* with me. I also miss the homecooked meals and laundry.

The front door opens and closes.

"Hello." Maziar's voice echoes from the foyer.

"We're in here," Mom calls back.

"Hi, Mom." Maziar wraps her up in a big bear hug as soon as he enters the kitchen, lifting her off her feet. She giggles like a child in his arms. "Hey," he directs toward me. His tone is clipped and strained, and I have to keep from scowling despite the sting.

"Hi," I reply, in much of the same manner.

Mom glances between the two of us, her eyebrows knitting together. But before she has a chance to ask what's going on, Sara steps in behind my brother.

"Hey."

"Hi, *aziz*," Mom responds, kissing both of Sara's cheeks.

There's an awkward pause as Mom decides whether she's going to start an inquisition, the worried look in her eyes all too familiar. I came to dinner tonight to tell my parents about Ramtin. Drama is definitive, but I'm not sure whether I'm ready to get into it while leaning against the kitchen island.

"Where's Dad?" I ask, changing the subject.

"He's in the shower. He'll be down in a minute," Mom answers.

I move over to the bowl sitting beside her and take the knife and cutting board out of her hands. Sara has already started washing the lettuce, placing it beside me to chop.

That sister-in-law of mine has some serious Spidey senses, always coming to my aid at the most necessary moments. She winks at me over Maziar's shoulder as she washes the rest of the salad vegetables, effectively moving Mom's attention back to dinner preparations. I nod my approval at her.

Judging from the way Maziar is staring me down, he's still not over the fact that I kicked him out of my house. Oh, well, his problem. That's what he gets for being an ass. I just ignore his silent wall of fury and go about my business as if I couldn't give two shits about his feelings.

The truth is, though, that having my relationship with my brother in shambles adds to the ever-growing knot sitting squarely in my stomach. I had hoped that when this conversation came around, he'd have my back. Sadly, he seems to be another hurdle I need to jump over.

"Hi, *dokhtaram*." Dad kisses my cheek, startling me out of my thoughts.

"Hi, Daddy," I say, leaning into his embrace. He smells of soap and aftershave. The familiarity causes a surge of panic to rush through my veins. *Please let them be on board. Please don't let them make me choose.*

I wish I didn't care about what they think, that I could go at this life thing alone. But I'm terrified about what they're going to say. For all the badass bitchiness I display for all to see, I really need my family's support.

Sara and I help Mom set the table while Maziar pops open a bottle of wine. Dad's already seated at the head. There's an exhaustion in the slump of his shoulders, complemented by his now almost white hair and deep crow's feet. He's just gotten a haircut, his scalp peeking through the pointy strands.

His age is blatantly mocking me, letting me know that my parents' lives are finite. For a moment, the realization strangles my heart, making it difficult to breathe. It's paralyzing watching Superman fall apart.

"What's wrong, *dokhtaram*?" His pale green eyes, a few shades lighter than my own, are emblazoned in his love for me.

"Nothing," I answer, kissing his cheek as I take the seat to his right.

Sara sits down beside me, squeezing my shoulder. She knows I'm about to drop the Ramtin bomb on the family; I had to tell someone. I was afraid if I didn't, I'd chicken out. But the time for backing away from reality has long left the station.

"How's everyone's week going?" Dad inquires, while scooping *baghalee polo, lima bean rice,* onto his plate.

"It's been good. Work's really busy," Maziar replies, shoving a spoonful of dinner in his mouth.

"How about you, *dokhtaram?*"

"Yeah, Bita. How has your week been going?" Maziar mocks. His mouth is partly filled with rice, but apparently, he just couldn't resist displaying his sarcasm.

I throw him an icy glare, clasping my hands together in my lap, unable to trust my impulses. Mom is sitting back observing yet another train wreck of an interaction between us.

"What's wrong with you two?" she asks. Her cheeks are flushed with irritation.

"Is something wrong?" Dad adds, looking up from his plate to find Maziar and me locked in a staring contest. He stumbles into silence, suddenly privy to the tension at the table.

"Maziar," Sara warns.

He doesn't bother looking at his wife. I'm sure he knows what side of the line she stands on, and I'm fairly certain it annoys the hell out of him. I smirk. I can't help myself. Big mistake because it only fuels Maziar's inferno.

"Why don't you ask your daughter why she kicked me out of her house last week?" he says.

Sara gasps, and I laugh, a maniacal rumble leaving my belly. I lean forward in my seat, never breaking eye contact. *He wants to play, so let's play.*

"Because little brother over here doesn't know how to mind his own business," I answer, not even waiting for Mom to ask the question.

"Guys, why don't we take a breath." Sara is a peacemaker at the fullest. I reach out and squeeze her hand resting on the table.

"It's okay, Sissy." I hear her exhale, knowing the shitstorm's about to hail on us. I turn toward Mom and Dad. "I've been dating Ramtin for the past five months." I don't twitch or flinch despite the ever-growing anxious spasms rushing through my limbs.

"Ramtin? Who's Ramtin?" Mom asks, not connecting the dots.

But Dad is much quicker than she is. "The real estate agent?"

"Yup. That Ramtin," Maziar responds for me.

"What does that have to do with kicking your brother out of your house?" Mom looks so confused, worry lines crisscrossing her forehead. Her eyes are wide with apprehension, but there's a curious glimmer nestled in her pupils. I grab hold and run with it.

"Maziar and Sara ran into us at a café. He showed up at the house a few days later to let me know he doesn't approve."

"Why don't you approve?" Mom turns toward him.

"What?" Maziar's voice is laced with the shock and confusion we're both experiencing at

Mom's nonchalant reaction.

I look at Dad, trying to size up how he feels about my confession. But he's cool and collected, as usual, giving nothing away. The knot that has begun to subside retightens in the pit of my stomach.

"What's your concern with your sister dating Ramtin, Maziar?" Dad asks.

"Really? Do I have to explain this to you guys?" He works the muscles of his jaw, and it makes me foolishly giddy. I know I shouldn't revel in the fact that Operation: Get Rid of Ramtin is unraveling before Maziar's eyes, but I can't help it.

"No need to be rude, Maziar," Mom chastises. "Dad's just asking what your thoughts are. We don't know Ramtin very well, so if you know something we don't, then we should talk about it."

Maziar huffs and Sara gives him a reassuring nod. He takes a deep breath before he begins to list the cons of my relationship. I have the urge to kick Sara under the table for showing him mercy. I'd prefer he feel that we're a family divided, us against him, so maybe he'd get off this soapbox of his. But then again, she's his wife, and despite how close we are, I have to accept that she won't be completely unsupportive of him. It doesn't stop me from wanting to reprimand her for it anyway.

"I have a couple issues with the idea of my sister dating this guy. First, he's forty-three. That's a fifteen-year gap between them."

"I can understand how that would be alarming to someone your age," Mom agrees. "But that was common in my time. Fifteen years isn't that horrible. Remember, Dad and I are ten years apart."

Maziar's jaw literally drops open at Mom's unconcerned reaction to our age difference. I totally get it, not having thought Mom would be on board, either. Nonetheless, I have to stifle a squeal at the way this conversation is shaping up.

"Okay," Maziar replies. "It's not just his age. He's also divorced." Mom cringes at the mention of Ramtin's ex. "And he has two kids." The figurative icing on the cake.

"Oh." Mom turns toward me. "How long has he been divorced?"

"Three years."

"And how old are his kids?"

"Fifteen and thirteen. And they're both girls." I preemptively answer the next question I know is coming.

"I see." She slowly leans back in her chair. "That could be a problem."

"It's not." I have no intention of letting them know I'm currently in some teenage feud with Yasi.

"Have you met his daughters?" Dad suddenly asks.

"Yes."

"And how has that gone?"

"It's been fine. They're kids. They just need some time to get used to the idea of their dad with another woman," I say. I realize if I make it seem all peachy, Yasi may blow my cover if she's ever around my family. This way, I can attribute her attitude to childish rebellion in response to her father's new relationship status.

"And what about the ex-wife?" Mom adds.

"She's fine, I guess. They really don't have much of a relationship other than when dealing with their daughters." *And when they do family breakfasts, and outings on the weekends, and when she thinks she has the right to show up at my house whenever she damn well pleases.*

Mom nods her head, deep in thought. I know she has more to say; I can see it in the concern painted across her crinkled eyelids and in the purse of her lips. At my age, I can easily find a man with less baggage. For Iranian parents, this isn't ideal, possibly a big disappointment in what they dreamed for me. But she doesn't say anything, having come a long way from the immediate outbursts and negation of Maziar and Sara's relationship. I don't know if the fact that Ramtin is Jewish makes this less of a blow for her than my brother's marriage.

I look at Sara wondering if Mom's evolution pleases her or makes her angry. I can understand if she feels either of those emotions. But she's too busy staring at Maziar, his cheeks puffed out in frustration. Sara's face is pale with concern, poised on the edge of her seat, ready to do damage control if Maziar loses it. I'm so flabbergasted by the series of events currently taking place at the table that I don't even bother to worry about what my brother will do next.

"Let's do dinner with Ramtin," Dad suggests. "If you're getting serious with this guy, we should meet him. Give him a chance before we pass any judgment." *When in the hell did my parents become so rational?* I have no idea, but I'll take it.

"Okay," I agree. I smile at Maziar, sweetly and lovingly, as I silently patronize him. Sara smacks my shoulder. I give her an apologetic grin.

"Let's eat," Dad says, shutting down the conversation.

Maziar grunts in response and puts another spoon full into his mouth, all the while staring daggers in my direction. Out of respect for my poor sister-in-law, who appears ill at her husband's angst, I divert my gaze back to my food and pretend I don't notice that Maziar is being a royal ass.

* * *

I fidget with the neckline of my blouse, making sure that it doesn't reveal too much cleavage. Oddly, it feels like I'm heading to an important job interview and too much boob would be unacceptable. In addition to that, Maziar has morphed into an old Iranian man. Tonight, I refuse to see his sidelong glances and disapproval on my less than modest outfit choice. It would be counterproductive.

I take one last glance in the full-length mirror, making sure my black slacks aren't wrinkled and my lavender top is tucked in evenly, before I head out of the bedroom.

Ramtin is sitting on my couch, his navy-blue trousers, fitted and sleek. The stark white dress shirt he sports is a perfect addition. His head is bowed as he scrolls through something on his phone, his elbows resting loosely on his knees. The image is magazine worthy as it takes my breath away. I sway with desire, battling the flurry of butterfly wings that encourage me to drop my clothes on the hardwood floor and make my way over to him naked.

"Hey," he says, when he notices me gawking. The grin that stretches across his lips only beckons me forward, pushing me to play hooky on this meet-and-greet dinner. "Are you ready?"

"Yes," I answer, desperately wanting to flake on the evening. But this isn't a family outing I can skip without serious repercussions.

I head over to the couch to grab my purse. He wraps his arms around my waist and pulls me onto his lap. His gaze is so deep that it tickles my soul. I can sense the urgency of words unsaid hovering on the tip of his tongue. My stomach flips in response. But he doesn't speak, instead leaning in and kissing me gently, allowing his body to do the talking. In the way he brushes the hair back from my face, and the soft touch of his lips on mine, I hear that he loves me. Maybe as much as I love him. To the point that it almost hurts.

"Let's go." He pulls away, leaving me breathless.

"Okay."

He opens the front door and allows me to pass through before stepping outside himself. As he uses his key to lock up, I can't help but imagine what it would feel like if we lived together permanently. The idea of waking up to Ramtin in my bed every morning makes me weak in the knees. I've never been this serious with a guy. No one else has met my parents.

But my daydream of playing house is abruptly halted when I think about how he hasn't given me a key to his place yet. Maybe he's afraid his daughters might show up unexpectedly? Or Roya? *Does she still have a key?* That wouldn't surprise me in the least.

I try to brush aside the negative emotions creeping into my thoughts. I convince myself that staying at my place is indeed a choice

I've made, and not one he's allowed me to because his life is too complicated. *It's more convenient for me to have him stay here. He leaves a few pairs of sweats and a toothbrush. I'd have to lug my entire wardrobe.*

"Ready?" he asks, stumbling me out of my thoughts.

"Yes, sorry." I'm unsure how long he's been watching me. I pull my lips into a broad smile, sure my cheeks are crimson with embarrassment.

"A lot on your mind. I get it. This dinner is a big deal."

He reaches out and grabs my hand, walking me over to the passenger side and opening the door. His chivalry still gives me goosebumps, making me feel like his princess.

We pull into the Nobu parking lot twenty minutes later. It dawns on me that this was the same place Mom and Dad had Maziar and Sara's meet-and-greet. Or at least the most important one, where Maziar put his foot down and refused to bend to Mom's will. How ironic that we'd be doing this at the same location. It makes me wonder if all life-altering conversations about future mates just have my parents gravitating toward sushi and the ocean.

The valet opens the door for me, but I sit glued to my seat, staring up at him in what I imagine is wide-eyed terror. It's irrational for me to be this scared; Mom and Dad didn't veto my relationship. As a matter of fact, they seemed somewhat onboard. Maziar is the only one sitting in full opposition, but I'm trusting that Sara can calm that storm. Nonetheless, I can't help but be afraid that this simple dinner in which my family wants to get to know my boyfriend, could combust into a million angry pieces. The sounds of the crashing waves and the serene sunset view don't stand a chance if this all goes sour.

The valet offers me his hand. He's young, no older than eighteen. His baby blues are watching me curiously, his eyelids harboring his confusion. He has no clue how monumental the next few hours will be, that they'll dictate whether it's smooth sailing or a full-on battle. He's too young to understand how complicated and messy life can get, with ex-wives and disgruntled brothers. I envy his naiveté.

I reach out and allow him to help me out of the car. He seems relieved that I'm not some nutcase he has to deal with on his shift. I almost laugh at the satisfied expression that claims his features.

Ramtin steps up beside me and gives me his arm. I rest my hand in the crook of his elbow and allow him to lead me inside. I spot my parents right away, seated out on the balcony next to the backdrop of the beautiful ocean.

"I see our party." I point in my family's direction and the hostess nods, giving us her consent to make our way over. When we reach the table, I lean in and hug my dad, kissing both his cheeks. "Hi, Daddy."

"Hi, *dokhtaram.*"

"*Salom,* Parviz *khan.*" Ramtin shakes my dad's hand. He isn't much younger than Dad, to be honest, a difference in years equal to ours, but Ramtin chooses to address my parents formally, showing his respect.

I kiss my mom and take the seat across from her, creating a protective barrier between Ramtin and my parents. He doesn't need it, he's a grown man, but I can't help it. I feel an urge to shield him from any negativity that may occur this evening. If the past is any indication, Mom may throw a curve ball. She was "on board" with meeting Sara, too, but then the she-devil reared her horrendous horns. I prefer to err on the side of caution.

"*Salom,* Naghemeh *khanoom.*" Ramtin leans across the table and kisses both Mom's cheeks before sitting down beside me. She smiles at him, but it doesn't reach her eyes, making my heart beat wildly against my ribcage.

"It's good to see you both again," Ramtin says, launching into casual conversation.

"You too, Ramtin," Dad replies. "How's work?"

"It's really good, actually. I've been very busy. Lots of showings."

"Are people buying a lot right now?" Mom asks. She tilts her head, playing innocent, but I know she's fishing for details on his income.

"Yes, it's a sellers' market at the moment." Ramtin doesn't let Mom's intrusion bother him. I, on the other hand, have to take a deep breath.

"Do you live near Bita?" she adds. She thinks she's being subtle, but she's not. With Mom, every question is calculated. She's gauging Ramtin's net worth. I have to force myself not to roll my eyes at her.

"I do," Ramtin answers. "I live a few blocks away. I bought my house three years ago after my divorce. It's in a nice neighborhood, and it's spacious. I wanted my daughters to be comfortable when they stayed with me." He gives her all the information upfront before she has a chance to ask him on her own. I'm surprised she doesn't follow it up by wanting square footage and market value.

I don't realize I'm rapidly tapping my leg beneath the table until Ramtin's hand rests on my knee. He continues to engage in conversation with my parents while silently confirming that he doesn't need my help.

The server steps up to take our drink order. *Alcohol. I so need that right now.* Just as he scribbles down Mom's Pepsi with no ice, Maziar and Sara appear at the table.

"Two vodka tonics, please," Maziar adds to the order, startling the server.

"No problem." He heads off to the bar.

Sara and Maziar greet us and take the last two seats at the table. Maziar places himself across from Ramtin in a power play. It doesn't intimidate Ramtin, but it irritates the hell out of me. Maziar seems happy with my reaction, and I reprimand myself for not controlling my features better. If he knows he's making me angry, he'll think he's already won.

Mom pulls the conversation back, wasting no time on the rooster dance Maziar seems adamant in engaging in. "You have two daughters. Is that right?"

"Yes. Yasi is fifteen and Kimiya is thirteen."

"How often do you see them?"

Dad sends Mom a cautionary glare. "I'm sorry for my wife's abruptness. We just want to get to know who our daughter is dating, that's all," he apologizes.

"Am I being rude?" Mom asks. Judging from the bewildered expression she wears, she really doesn't think launching immediately into an interrogation two minutes after Ramtin is seated at the table is bad manners.

I open my mouth to tell her that indeed she's forgotten social etiquette, when Ramtin's hand squeezes my knee in warning. The smile never leaves his face and he doesn't break eye contact with Mom.

Despite not looking at me, apparently, he's gauging my energy, each silent gesture imploring me to keep it together.

"No, Naghmeh *khanoom*. This is what the dinner is for. All you and Parviz *khan* know of me is what I've done as your real estate agent. It makes complete sense that you'd want to know more about me now." Mom sports a girlish grin. For a minute, she appears to swoon. Relief floods my insides. "I share custody with my ex-wife, Roya. We live a few blocks away from each other, so the girls don't have to be displaced very far each time they travel back and forth. It's another reason why I bought my house. My kids can literally walk from one house to the other."

Mom's politely smiling but it wavers, her lips pressing into a thin line. I wish he'd left their proximity out.

"How does Roya feel about the two of you?" Maziar throws in. Now I do roll my eyes.

"She's fine with it. We've moved on and are just friends." Ramtin takes it in stride. I want to reach out and punch Maziar.

"Have you met her, Bita?"

"Yup," I say, glaring at my brother for his unyielding desire to rock the boat.

"How about the girls?" he continues. "How do they feel about their father dating a much younger woman?"

"Maziar," Dad scolds.

"What?" he asks, feigning innocence. "Kids have a tough time when their parents date other people. And look, it can't be easy for your fifteen-year-old to watch her dad be with someone that looks almost her own age."

This time, I don't let Ramtin's death grip on my knee stop me. It's almost like he's trying to hold me in place, knowing all too well I'm about to launch myself across the table.

"What the hell is wrong with you?" I growl.

"Bita!" Mom gasps.

Maziar leans back in his seat with a smug expression. This is the classic way things go down around here; Maziar is the dick and I get in trouble for my retaliation. *Well, screw that!* I'm done playing these traditional familial roles. It's time they change because I'm not doing this anymore.

"What?" I turn to glower at Mom. She wasn't expecting me to challenge her as shock slackens her features. "He's being a jerk, and I'm the one you're concerned with?"

Maziar's smirk grows wider.

"Maziar, knock it off," Dad demands. "Ramtin, I'm sorry for my family's behavior." He shakes his head, an apologetic softness in his eyes. His tired expression reminds me that he's been here before, stuck between two people he loves as they draw lines in the sand.

"I'm sorry, Daddy." His hands are resting on the table and I reach out and wrap my fingers around them. I feel bad for my dad, but I can't let the guilt quiet me down like it's done so many times before. "Really, what is your issue right now?" I ask, directing my attention to Maziar. "Why do you care so much about how much younger I am or what I have to deal with?" My tone is even but there's no mistaking my fury. Either Maziar treads lightly in his cause, or I'm leaving this dinner, and my brother, behind.

Sara is sitting to Ramtin's right, and at this point, her face has paled, and she looks ill. The familiar expression of worry she seems to wear frequently these days tightens her features. When I glance at Ramtin, the hard press of his lips tells me he's disappointed in how I'm handling the situation. It makes my stomach churn and I suddenly sympathize with Sara. I need to reel back the tension so this dinner isn't a total failure. And judging from how silent and unyielding Ramtin is, I may have another battle when I get home.

"Let me try that again," I say. "I appreciate your concern, but I don't understand why you're so upset about it all." Ramtin gently rubs my knee in approval. *Thank God. I'm in no mood to fight with him too.*

"Because you have no idea what you're doing!" Apparently Maziar didn't get the memo that we're trying to calm it all down.

"And you know what I'm doing?"

"You're going to get hurt. You just don't see it. You're too busy being wrapped up in this love thing to realize you're setting yourself up to have your heart broken," he explains.

I look at my brother leaning forward in his seat, his hands clasped tightly together, worry lines framing his eyes, and I feel sorry for him. He's so tangled in his own anger to realize we've done this before. The only difference is that last time, he was me and Mom was him. I shake my head.

"I understand why you'd be worried," Ramtin says, taking the lead. I lean back in my seat, allowing him to, because I need a moment to gather my thoughts. Maziar's reaction just confuses me. "I have a lot of baggage. But I love your sister, and I'd never do anything to hurt her."

"We appreciate that." Dad takes back control of the conversation. "I'm sure you can understand Maziar's concern for his sister. All of our concern," he clarifies. "We just don't want Bita to get her hopes up for something that won't last. Relationships are hard enough as it is. When you add the extra elements, it just gets more difficult to deal with. That's all. You seem like a really great guy. But can you guarantee things will work out?"

Before Ramtin has a chance to answer, I jump back in. "There's no way to guarantee it. You all know that. What you're asking is ridiculous." Ramtin's fingers squeeze my knee again and I huff, trying to fight the urge to swat his hand away.

"I can guarantee that my family isn't going to be a problem. That's what you're asking, right?"

Dad nods and blinks his approval, seemingly content at Ramtin's response.

"But why even start something this complicated?" *Maziar just won't quit!*

"Maziar, I think that's enough worrying for tonight," Mom cuts him off.

"I agree with your mother. I think that your sister and Ramtin are capable of figuring this out on their own."

Maziar sits back in his seat, dejected, as if my parents' support of my relationship is some unfathomable betrayal. *This can't really be about my relationship, could it?* It feels like there's something more. I want to let it go, get through this awful dinner and head home, but I'm so baffled and thrown off by his reaction that I can't help myself.

"I'm so disappointed in you," I confess. Maziar's expression darkens, but Sara puts her hand on his forearm to steady him. "We've been here, in this exact place, at this very table, I think."

"No, it was two tables down," Sara corrects. We exchange regretful glances, Mom joining in. Not one of our finer moments.

"This conversation has happened before. Maybe the players and details are different, but it's the same. If I remember correctly, you couldn't understand how any of us were allowing our own feelings to cloud our judgment. And you weren't having it, because you loved Sara, and no one was going to tell you that you couldn't be with her," I say. "It wasn't that long ago, Maziar. Have you already forgotten?" I feel the tears lodged in my throat. I hated fighting with my brother then, and I hate it now. The fact that he doesn't want this for me is breaking my heart.

"It's not the same thing," Maziar assures me.

"Yes, it is," Sara protests.

He looks between his wife and me, then down at my parents. The tension in his shoulders lessens as he faces Ramtin. "I love my sister," he admits. "I just don't want her to get hurt."

"I love your sister, too. And I won't hurt her."

"I'm going to hold you to that," Maziar warns. Ramtin nods. They make a silent pact, and then Maziar raises his hand to get the server's attention. "Can we get another round, please? And some menus."

"Of course." The server nods, then heads back to the bar.

"Let's eat," Dad adds.

Mom, Sara, and I lean back in our seats simultaneously exhaling. The first battle has successfully been won. As Maziar gives me a defeated smile, I pray the war is over.

CHAPTER ELEVEN

I shrug out of my white coat, attempting to untangle myself from the expensive magnifying glasses hanging around my neck. Normally, they help me see while sitting in an upright ergonomic position, but they're currently in the process of attacking me. I pull at the cord, but it won't disconnect from the attached LED light.

"Ugh!" I groan, caught in a ridiculous spider web.

Once free, I hurriedly drop everything on my desk and turn to run to the bathroom when my office phone rings.

"Damn it!" I fumble with the receiver, my bladder protesting the delay. Too many patients this morning made for multiple cups of coffee devoured and zero bathroom breaks taken. "Yes," I answer, now bouncing on my toes.

"Doctor Hakimi, you have line two."

"Who is it?" I whine.

"Ramtin."

"Okay." *Why is he calling me at work?* "Hey," I say, switching over to his call. "Everything okay?"

"Sorry to call your office, but you weren't picking up your cell."

I notice my phone hidden beneath a pile of charts. I was so

preoccupied with needing to pee that I forgot to check it. I pick it up to find two missed calls.

"Oh, sorry. Busy morning. What's up?"

"I hate to ask you this, but are you going on your lunch break right now?"

"Yeah, why?"

"I need a huge favor," he begs. "They just called from Yasi's school. She's sick and needs to be picked up. I'm in the middle of a showing and can't leave, and Roya is in Pasadena. She's trying to get back, but she's stuck in traffic." He pauses and my stomach knots up with the question I know is coming. "Is there any way you could pick her up and drop her off at my house? Roya is heading there now."

Shit! I don't want to pick her up! "Will they release her to me?" I'm hoping the logistics will save me.

"Yes. If you can do it, I just have to call them and let them know you're coming. They'll ask to see your ID, but that's it."

"Okay," I agree, hesitantly.

"Thanks, *eshgham*. You're a lifesaver." He sounds so relieved I feel guilty for the dread I'm battling. "I love you."

"I love you, too."

"I'm going to make this up to you," he assures, a playful tone in his voice. My skin tingles at the innuendo.

"I'm going to hold you to it," I tease.

"I'm counting on it." I hear the mischievous smirk on his lips. "I'll see you later tonight."

"See you later," I answer. "Bye."

"Bye, *eshgham*." He hangs up and the dread settles deeper into the pit of my stomach.

I have to deal with the Persian princess, and I can think of a hundred other things I'd rather do. Like pee. And eat, since it's my lunch break. Now, I'm forced to take a teenage beating in the next hour and return to the chaos of the afternoon starving. *Lovely.*

I grab my purse off the chair. Bathroom break first, Little Miss Diva afterwards.

I park in front of Yasi's school fifteen minutes later. The nurse's office is to the right of the entrance, clearly marked, making it easy to spot.

"Hi, I'm here to pick up Yasi Kahen," I announce.

The nurse looks up from her computer, her face framed by long strands of wavy gray hair. She's wearing reading glasses low on her nose, her pale blue eyes kind and comforting. Wrinkles consume her skin as she smiles. She's a picturesque rendition of a sweet old grandmother, exactly what's necessary in a school nurse.

"Miss Hakimi?" she asks.

"Yes. Sorry. Here's my ID," I say, rummaging through my purse for my wallet.

Once I've adequately confirmed my identity, she gives me a satisfied nod.

"Yasi, dear, your ride is here," she calls over her shoulder.

Yasi steps out from a room I didn't notice off to the side. She's in a pair of fitted light-blue jeans and a dark gray tank top. There's an oversize maroon sweatshirt awkwardly tied around her waist. It's bearlike in comparison to her long thin frame. It looks like it's swallowing her whole.

"Great, it's you," she declares, rolling her eyes.

The nurse raises one brow in question.

"Yup, it's me," I reply. My tone is chipper as I state the obvious, winning me a scrunched-up nose and a teenage dirty look. I'm hoping the fake smile stretched across my face hides my irritation. I'd have to be a moron not to notice Yasi's blatant rudeness, but for some reason, I have the strange urge to save face in front of Grandma. "Thank you," I mumble to the nurse, then spin on my heels and walk into the hallway.

I don't turn around to see if Yasi is following, because I really don't care. Less than five minutes into our interaction, I already want to leave her to wait for Roya on the curb. But the shuffle of her feet indicates that she's close behind.

The bell rings, shrill and loud, startling me. Classroom doors swing open and students pour out into the hallways, the sound of their chatter echoing off the walls. It intensifies the headache I'm nursing. I pinch my nose and stop to scan the area, making sure I haven't lost

Yasi. Despite being annoying as hell, losing her before the mission is complete wouldn't bode well with the boyfriend.

She's standing a few feet away from me. I go to call her name but stop short when I realize she's staring wide-eyed at a group of boys that have just exited the door directly in front of her. The crimson hue of embarrassment flushes her skin and her eyes well up with tears. The boys are snickering, pointing at her and laughing. I can't hear what they're saying over the loud hum of voices, but judging from the quiver of Yasi's lip, it isn't good.

Without thinking, I launch into motion, taking four big strides until I'm beside her. I flash the boys a cautionary warning, stopping them mid-taunt. Yasi is frozen in the moment, unaware of me or the crowd around her. She just stares, at one boy in particular, hurt and despair written in her expression. He notices her watching him, and for a second, the sneering smirk and bullying vibe lose their momentum. His expression transforms into regret but lasts mere seconds before his heckling friends get the best of him.

"Let's get out of here," he orders. He spares Yasi one more glance before turning and leaving her in his shadow. His entourage follows obediently, laughing hysterically.

Yasi turns toward me. "I really want to get out of here," she pleads. Her voice is a quiet whisper as she forces the words from her lips. I can imagine there's a momentous knot lodged in her throat, making it impossible to speak.

"Sure." I place my hand on her back and try to guide her through the thick crowd. She doesn't flinch or bat my hand away as she normally would. Instead, she allows me to help her.

Once outside, we make our way over to the car in silence. Her eyes are bloodshot from trapped tears and her lips are pulled into a frown. She sits in the passenger seat, her long frame crumbling in on itself as she protectively crosses her arms over her chest.

"Boys can be real jerks sometimes," I say.

As I pull out of the school parking lot, I make sure to keep my gaze trained on the road. I don't want to make an already tense situation worse. I get the feeling that too much direct attention will only aggravate her further. It wouldn't surprise me if she were to take her frustration out on me, so I tread carefully.

"You can say that again," she mumbles. She's staring out the passenger window as she reaches down and tightens the sweatshirt around her waist.

Suddenly, it dawns on me.

"They really are insensitive. I think it's in their nature. But they don't get what it means to be a girl."

I'm not entirely sure I have the situation pegged, but she hasn't told me to shut up just yet, so I take that to mean she's too broken down by the day's events to dislike me as much as she usually does. That hate is claimed by others today.

"I got my period pretty late in comparison to my friends," I begin. She shuffles uncomfortably in her seat but doesn't stop me. I push forward. "I think it was the end of my freshman year. So, when I started tenth grade, I was still getting used to gauging when it was coming. I don't know about you, but I was irregular."

"Yeah, me too," she confirms. She's staring straight ahead now, big childlike eyes dominating her face. I suddenly realize how young she is. Her attitude usually renders her older. She's far from the confident, unyielding kid I'm used to, and I find it jarring.

"I can't even remember now how far into the school year it was, but I think it may have just been a few weeks," I continue. "I was wearing these new white jeans my mom had just bought me and a light blue off-the-shoulder top. I thought I looked so good," I emphasize. She's all ears, unconsciously leaning in my direction, her features frozen in anticipation of what's about to come. "The day was over, and I was heading to my mom's car. I had to walk through to the back of the school to get to her."

"What happened?" she asks in a whisper, when I don't continue right away. I have her hooked, just as I'd hope.

"These two loser boys start laughing and pointing at me. At first, I had no idea what was going on. I feel stupid saying this now, but I didn't know they were making fun of me. I thought maybe one was pointing me out to the other because he thought I was hot. But the more they laughed, I figured out something was wrong."

Yasi's shaking her head in disbelief. I know she's thinking back to the boys in the hall doing the same snickering and pointing as I'm describing now.

"I started freaking out because I didn't know what was going on, so I ran like hell to my mom's car. But it wasn't until I got home that I realized what the fuss was all about." I pull to a stop at a red traffic light and turn to face her, hoping she can see the camaraderie and sincerity I'm attempting to convey with my story. She's still not facing me but her gaze flashes in my direction. "There was a big bloodstain on my butt."

"Oh my God," Yasi gasps, finally turning toward me. "Your white jeans?" I nod. "Guys are such assholes!" Fury dances in her pupils at the injustice.

"Assholes, indeed," I agree, not bothering to tell her not to curse. Sometimes, life just needs words like asshole and douchebag.

She takes in a sharp inhale and lets it out slowly. I can see the conundrum brewing inside her. Does she let down her walls, giving into the shared vulnerability between her and the woman she's proclaimed as her archnemesis? Or does she tell me to buzz off, trashing my attempt at softening our relationship? For the first time, I feel sorry for her. Not only for what horrific events have muddled her day, but for the tough spot she's been in these past few months while her father moves on with a new woman. A much younger woman, for that matter.

"Did you see the tall guy with the green shirt?" she finally asks.

I nod as I put the car back in drive, heading to her dad's house. Her trust is making me giddy, but I steady my features, knowing it would ruin the somber moment.

"His name is Charlie. I thought he liked me, but he was the first to start making fun of me today." A muffled sob escapes her lips.

I have the urge to reach out and squeeze her hand, but I'm afraid she'll recoil at my touch and the moment will be lost. So, instead, I stay glued at ten and two, glancing in her direction every few seconds so she knows I'm listening.

"What a jerk."

"Yeah," she agrees.

I pull into Ramtin's driveway and turn the car off. Yasi doesn't hurriedly get out, so I stay seated quietly beside her in hopes that she has more to share with me.

"He kissed me a few weeks ago at a friend's birthday party." Tears well up in her eyes again but this time, she lets them fall. Her openness and vulnerability pull at my heartstrings and I feel a strong desire to turn the car around, find this Charlie character, and give him a proper beating. "It was my first kiss," she admits. "I really like him." She drops her face into her hands and begins to cry.

I reach out this time and rub gentle circles on her back. "It'll be okay. Charlie is just an idiot," I insist. "And sadly, he won't be the last idiot you meet. Most boys are just stupid." That earns me a small giggle and a snort. "But then one day, you'll meet that special boy who makes your heart beat wildly in your chest, and every time he's around, it's hard to breathe. That boy will be special, and you won't even remember Charlie anymore."

"Is that what it's like with my dad?" She turns her face in her hands to stare up at me. Her eyelashes are damp with tears, her skin red and blotchy from the crying. But there's something new glimmering in her expression. Hope. For her, or for her father and me, I don't really know, but it's burning as bright as day.

"Yes. Only so much more." I smile. The flicker of my own hopefulness takes shape. The possibility that I may win over the daughter of the man I love beats uncontrollably in my chest.

Suddenly, a black Mercedes pulls in behind me, boxing me into the driveway. *Roya. Great.* She makes it over to the passenger side in seconds, yanking the car door open. When she sees Yasi's tearstained face, she proceeds to aggressively yank her daughter out of her seat.

"What did you say to her?" she accuses, hugging Yasi to her chest.

"What?" Her erratic behavior throws me off, and I don't put the pieces together right away. Not until Yasi jumps in, wiggling out of her mom's embrace.

"She didn't do anything," Yasi answers.

Roya looks at Yasi's tired, broken expression and assumes the worst. She grabs hold of her daughter's shoulders as she makes her plea. "Yasi, don't be afraid of this woman. We tell each other everything, remember. If she's done something to upset you, then tell me," she urges.

"No, Mom," Yasi asserts, pulling away from Roya. "I'm not afraid of Bita, and she didn't do anything. I leaked on my pants and some stupid boys made fun of me. Bita was actually helping." She huffs and rolls her eyes at her mother's ridiculousness. "Thanks for the ride, Bita," she mutters, before abruptly turning and heading to the Mercedes.

Roya stares at her daughter's departure, shock settled in her features. When she turns back to face me, anger lines crisscross her forehead. *Apparently, it's time for a Botox reboot.*

She doesn't say anything, but I get the distinct feeling she's sizing up her competition. What she doesn't understand is that there is no competition. I may not have won over her children just yet, but today was definite progress. But as far as Ramtin is concerned, I've already won that battle. She's had her chance to deal with her regrets.

I'm about to tell her to back off, struggling with the profanity sitting aggressively on my tongue, when I notice Yasi watching us from the car. Getting into an argument with her mom would ruin all the headway we've made this afternoon. Instead, I choose to stay silent. I almost pat myself on the back for being such a mature adult.

"Thanks for picking Yasi up," Roya finally offers, then quickly turns on her heels and goes to her car. I watch as she pulls out of the driveway and can't help but feel a little victorious when Yasi gives me a small wave.

As I make my way back to work, I realize it's been a very good day. I created bonds with Yasi and annoyed the hell out Roya. Definitely a win in my book.

CHAPTER TWELVE

I'm struggling with the keys and the three grocery bags draped over my shoulder, when Maziar's BMW pulls into the driveway.

"Great," I mumble. It's been a long week and I'm too tired for brotherly advice. Or rather, brotherly directive orders.

Since the meet-and-greet with my family, Maziar has backed off enough that he's not showing up at my house to tell me he disagrees with my life choices. But he also hasn't called. This week has been radio silent.

I have no idea what version of my brother I'll be encountering this afternoon, as he unfolds his broad shoulders from the car. He pulls two brown Del Taco bags out of his front seat and I wonder if he's brought a peace offering or a last meal. When he attempted to bring a fast-food remedy to our previous sibling squabble, I ended up kicking him out of my house.

I step inside and drop the grocery bags on the kitchen counter, leaving the front door open for Maziar to follow. I hear him swing it shut and feel trepidation lace through my veins, squeezing my organs. When he walks into the kitchen, I try to even my expression, hoping to hide the fact that I wish he'd called first.

"Hey," he says. "I brought lunch."

He lifts the bags up in front of him, sheepishly pulling his lower lip between his teeth, and the clenched fist around my heart loosens just a little. *Maybe this won't be so bad.* Or maybe I just have no defenses against this man, and I'll be blindsided again.

"Thanks," I reply. "I'm starving." His smile deepens as I accept his offering. "Let me just get these groceries in the fridge before they go bad."

He places the bags down on the kitchen island. "Let me help," he offers.

We work side by side for the next ten minutes, trying to shove all the food I bought into my undersize refrigerator. It's a bad game of Tetris that leaves Maziar talking crap and me laughing hysterically as he cusses out the milk carton. The tension I felt when he first pulled up has dissipated, and I've almost forgotten that we're stuck in a serious disagreement.

Despite Maziar having a moment of understanding with Ramtin at dinner, I know my brother, and I know he still harbors his opinions. I'm also aware that he's come here to tell me all about them. But being stuck in a battle of wills with him leaves me feeling out of place and anxious, so I'm hoping that today's conversation will help us smooth out the edges of our relationship.

"The tacos are probably soggy now," Maziar predicts, as he empties the contents of the bags onto the kitchen table. He has enough food to feed at least five people, and sadly, I'm pretty sure there'll be no leftovers once we're done.

"Please. They just taste better that way anyway," I encourage, popping open two cans of Coke as I make my way to the seat opposite him. He responds with a childish grin, and I'm reminded of when we were younger.

I forget that despite Maziar's macho-Iranian exterior, I'm still his older sister, and he cares what I think. It's hard to remember sometimes, when he acts like such an intolerable ass, that when there's unrest between us, that it's not just my world that feels rocked at the core.

He takes a big bite of a taco, and juice runs down the side of his chin. His puffed cheeks make me giggle, and the fist clenched in my stomach disappears altogether. I watch my brother, enjoying the greasy deliciousness before us, and feel a pang of sadness. He's so important to me, and it kills me to think that I may have to choose. I love Ramtin, but I love Maziar, too.

"What?" he asks, when I continue staring.

"What's going on with you?"

"What do you mean?" He puts the taco down and wipes his mouth, folding his hands in front of him when he's done. His energy shifts, becoming somber.

"You know what I mean. Why are you so angry with me?"

"I'm not angry." He's lying, averting his gaze to the bay windows.

"I know you," I comfort, placing my hand on his. "I know you're angry, but I honestly have no idea why. I get that you don't think dating Ramtin is a good idea because of his age and the kids, but you're actually pissed. Not just irritated with my choices, like I'd expect you to be."

He shakes his head but doesn't speak.

"Talk to me, Maziar," I urge.

He turns back to face me but pauses. I can see a mixture of ego and vulnerability competing in his furrowed brow.

"Come on. We've always been able to talk about anything." The anger I had felt a week ago has whittled down to nothingness, as his true feelings become transparent. There's so much more here than just a boyfriend he dislikes, and I'm determined to understand what.

He exhales, slowly and purposefully, before he begins to speak. "You always care what I think."

"I do," I agree, confused.

"This is the first time you haven't told me about a guy you're dating," he continues. "And the first time you don't give a shit about what I say."

"That's not true."

"Isn't it?" he asks. "Why didn't you tell me about Ramtin?"

As I look at my brother, sitting before me, hurt and neglected, I truly see how important I am to him. For the first time, I realize that I have a bigger hold on him than I thought I did. I always felt like the relationship was one-sided, that I needed him more than he needed me. But in this moment, I know I've been wrong.

I'm transported back to when Maziar chose Sara over his family, and how that broke my heart. I don't want to make him feel that way. Ever.

"I'm so sorry," I apologize.

"I don't need an apology. I just want to understand when it was that you thought you couldn't trust me."

"I do trust you." My voice is hoarse, pushing against the knot that has formed in my throat.

"No, you don't. If you did, I wouldn't have found out about Ramtin when I accidentally ran into you guys."

My eyes well up with tears, and Maziar squeezes my hand. He smiles, sad and forced, but he does it anyway because he knows I need him to. I need him to silently confirm that we haven't ruined the most important relationship to us both.

"I'm sorry. I don't know why I didn't tell you. I think I was just scared. I really care about Ramtin, and I knew you wouldn't be happy about it."

"I knew you wouldn't be happy about Sara, either, but I told you."

"You're right. You did tell me," I admit. *I have officially won the suckiest sister award.* "I should have told you."

"Yes, you should have." He laughs. "We won't always agree, but that's okay. You still need to talk to me."

"Why didn't you just tell me that to begin with?"

"Because I'm a guy and didn't want to admit that my sister could make me cry," he jokes.

"Did I make you cry?" I gape.

"On the inside," he answers. This time I laugh.

"Liar. I made you all weepy," I tease. He playfully rolls his eyes.

"But seriously," he continues. "I hate feeling like I don't matter to you. When I found out that you'd kept Ramtin from me, it felt like I'd lost you somehow."

"You'll never lose me," I protest.

"I know. It sounds stupid and lame. But I can't help it. That's just what it felt like."

"I'm sorry, Maziar."

"Thanks. And I'm sorry that I didn't support you like I should have," he admits. "I need to do better."

"Me, too."

He squeezes my hand one more time. "Now, can we get back to our really soggy tacos?" he whines.

"Absolutely." I unwrap one from the pile and take the biggest bite I can hold in my mouth. Grease dribbles down my chin, earning me a deep chuckle.

"I love you, Maziar."

"I love you too, Sis."

And just like that, all is right in the world again.

* * *

"So, you guys worked it out?" Ramtin asks.

"Yeah." I'm giddy at the recent progress I've made on both family fronts.

"That's great." His eyelashes are thick and black over the rim of his whiskey glass as he takes a sip.

"It is. I'm just happy we're back to normal," I confess. "Being out of sorts with Maziar always throws me off." I lift my wine glass to my lips as I scan the restaurant. It's a pretty quiet night for a Saturday, only a handful of tables occupied by patrons, making it easy to have a conversation without competing with a loud crowd.

"I can tell."

"Really?"

"Yes. As it should. He's your brother, so it makes sense." Ramtin runs his thumb gently down the side of my face. "I'm glad you're happy, *eshgham*."

I lean into his hand, breathing in the feel of his fingertips on my skin. Goosebumps rise across my flesh, the common reaction to his touch. He's watching me with mischief dancing in his eyes, completely exposing the thoughts running through his mind.

"How about we get out of here?" I suggest. "I say we take this celebration to your place."

His expression clouds over momentarily, his eyebrows twitching to be pulled to the middle of his face. But he regains his composure and quickly returns to his playful grin.

"We're celebrating?"

He nonchalantly glides over my suggestion of going to his house, while watching me with hunger embedded deep in his pupils, seductively running his tongue across his lower lip. I almost lose my train of thought as I revel in the idea of him devouring me whole.

"Why don't we ever go to your place?"

The question throws Ramtin off his game, because he stumbles when he says, "We do go to my house."

"I don't mean hanging out for a few hours or stopping by your place for a minute. I mean why don't we ever stay the night in your bed instead of mine?" I've completely ruined the heated desire we shared moments ago, replacing it with an uncomfortable tension.

When it becomes clear I won't be letting this go, Ramtin reaches out and grabs my hand from across the table. The gesture makes me nervous despite his intention.

"It's just easier to be at your place," he explains. "When we're at mine, I'm always worried my daughters will barge in."

"But we aren't even together on your weekends," I point out.

"I know. But my kids have the key to my house. And I live only a few blocks from Roya. That was done by design, so the girls didn't have to feel tied down by custody rights. If they want to see me, or if they forgot something at my house, they just come over."

There are so many immature things I want to say. *Why can't they call, knowing you have a girlfriend now?* Or, *things have changed; when it's not their weekend, it's mine, and they should respect that, as I respect their time with you.* But I don't say any of it, because I know how childish and ridiculous I'd sound. His reasoning is sound. And it isn't about me, not really. I can understand why he doesn't want his daughters walking in on our heated sexcapades. I don't, either. So instead, I do a little distracting myself, pulling the conversation back to our previous, more enjoyable topic. Sex.

"Fair enough," I answer. I shove the boulder sitting squarely in my chest, as far down as I can until it is barely a nuisance tickling my subconscious. "As for whether we're celebrating, yes, we are." I coyly twist a strand of hair between my fingers, and he responds with desire flaming in his eyes once again.

"What are we celebrating?" His grin pulls up tighter at the edges.

"Mending my relationship with my brother," I say. "And building a small bridge with Yasi." At the mention of his daughter, Ramtin's expression morphs into a full-blown smile, exposing all of his amazing teeth. The dentist in me can't help but notice how perfectly aligned and starkly white they are. The wings in my chest flap harder.

"Well, that definitely sounds like a reason to celebrate," he replies. "Let's get out of here." He winks, and every nerve ending in my body buzzes to life.

It's not until Ramtin is breathing deeply beside me, in my bed, that the pang of apprehension returns to my chest. His arm is stretched across my stomach, the other curved under the pillow beneath his head. His breath flutters against my cheek, even and calm, a contradiction to my current mental state. The familiar shape of my light fixture taunts me from overhead, emphasizing how we never made it to his place. I stifle a groan.

I carefully shimmy out from beneath Ramtin's hold, turning onto my side to gaze out the window. It's almost two in the morning, the streets dark except for the cone-shaped beams that brighten the sidewalk every few feet. My heart beats restlessly in my chest, and I have the sudden urge to go out for a walk. It's too late for all of that, so I resort to getting out of bed for a glass of water.

I cinch my robe in tighter, the cold marble tiles of the kitchen floor sending a hollow chill up my spine. I fill my glass and sit in the nook, staring out onto the street at nothing. A despondency settles in my shoulders.

At the start of the night, I was floating with my most current wins. But the more I think about it, I'm not so sure they mean anything. Does one moment with Yasi, or one conversation with Maziar, truly show that this can all work out? Especially when there's a nagging voice constantly giving me the feeling that despite Ramtin's love for me, he still keeps me at arm's length where his family is concerned. Will I ever truly fit into his life?

Will there be a time when our worlds melt into one? When he and his daughters will join in on my parent's Hanukkah celebration, and when we pull out folding tables on Thanksgiving to accommodate our newly expanded family? Or will his custody weekends continue to dictate when and if I'll see him? And even more concerning, if he's not with me, will he be with Roya? The questions whirl around my mind long after the water in my glass has disappeared.

"Are you okay?"

I yelp, startled.

"Sorry, I didn't mean to scare you," Ramtin apologizes.

He's leaning against the door frame, arms crossed over his bare chest, each muscle along the length of him fiercely defined. A sleepy grin settles on his lips as his eyes run the length of me, down my face, my neck, onto the skin of my exposed chest. His desire, even at three in the morning, feels heavy and yearning from across the room.

I want to ask him what's happening between us, how this will all play out if indeed we have this future I've dreamt up in my head. But the words are lost on the tip of my tongue, evaporated by fear. So instead, I sashay slowly in his direction, each sway of my hips sultry by design. When I finally stand before him, his hooded gaze peers down on me like fingertips running across my heated skin.

My robe has loosened, exposing the nakedness I wear beneath it. When Ramtin reaches out and pulls the edge of its fabric, allowing the entire thing to glide onto the tiles, I let him, wanting nothing more than to use his body to get out of my own head. I lean into him, my breast teasing his chest. His heart beats against my own, two rhythms that sync in the darkness.

I lift up on my tiptoes and kiss him, taking the tender flesh of his lips between my teeth. His breath becomes ragged and his need for me presses against my thigh. A wave of desire flushes my skin as I take him between my hands and hear him groan against my mouth.

Unable to control his lust any longer, he grabs me by the waist and carries me back to the bedroom. I wrap my legs tightly around him, my lips leaving trails of hot kisses across his neck. When he lays me down, staring deeply into my eyes, I have to force myself not to look away, my fears and apprehensions pushing to the surface again. To lose Ramtin would be devastating. This much I'm sure of.

I can't help but wonder if all I stand to lose, all I must give up in order to be with him, is worth the weight of my possible regret? A past I can't break into; a future that's uncertain. A daughter who's fickle with her feelings; a brother desperate for my attention. And a family of my own that may never come to life.

When he leans down and presses his lips against mine, oblivious to the war waging on inside me, I allow him to muddle my thoughts with his touch, to quiet the noise with his fingertips as they caress my body with perfection. And when he enters inside of me, I give in to my desire, letting my physical need drown out my emotional doubts.

Somewhere between darkness and daybreak, I fall asleep with my head on Ramtin's chest, the melodic beating of his heart my own personal lullaby. I use it to shut down the voices protesting in my mind, too exhausted with the future and all its "what ifs" to address them any longer tonight. Instead, as I flutter off to the land of dreams, I send a prayer for a tiny sign.

CHAPTER THIRTEEN

"Can't you just set something up?" Shiva asks. She's lying across my couch, curled beneath a throw blanket.

"Didn't he give you his number?"

"Yeah."

"Well, why don't you just call him?"

"Because then he'll know I'm into him!" Shiva throws her arm over her eyes in frustration.

"Isn't that the point?" I love messing with her.

"No! I want him to be into me first. Can't you just make it happen?"

"I mean, I guess I could." She throws a pillow at me just as I begin to giggle.

"I don't like your level of commitment, Bita," she teases.

"I'm not even that close to him," I admit. The fact that I've seen Kian on only a few occasions confirms my lack of involvement in Ramtin's life.

"He could totally be the one. I can feel it. There's potential there."

I smile at Shiva's confidence.

"You could be helping marry me off," she adds.

"Okay, okay." I laugh. "Let me talk to Ramtin." I roll onto my side, lying across the couch facing hers, and wrap my arm over my stomach as a wave of nausea threatens to make me sick on the living room floor.

"What's wrong with you?"

"I don't know. I think I ate something bad," I groan.

"Like food poisoning?"

"Maybe."

"Do you feel like throwing up?" she says.

"Yeah." I breathe deeply, as I'm flooded with nausea yet again. It's been happening on and off for the past few hours.

"But we ate the same thing for breakfast," Shiva replies, shifting her body until she's sitting up facing me. The throw blanket pools around her waist showing off its cinched appearance.

My hand unconsciously makes its way to my belly, running my fingers across its bloated exterior. "I don't feel so good."

Shiva's watching me, her head tilted to the side as she eyes me carefully.

"What?" When she doesn't reply, I add, "Why are you looking at me like that?" I have no idea why the crazy flutter of nerves joins the waves of nausea, but the way she's staring at me makes me uneasy.

"When did you get your period last?" she asks.

"The twelfth. Why?"

"It's the twentieth today," she states.

The blood drains from my face as I sit up to face her. "I'm late." I hadn't even thought about it until now.

"You're a week late, to be exact. Is that normal for you?"

"No." I shake my head, trying to dislodge the possibility that I could be pregnant from my reality.

"Oh, shit. That's not good," Shiva confirms the obvious.

"No, it's not."

"Should we get a pregnancy test or something?" she asks. "Isn't that what you're supposed to do?"

"I don't know what I'm supposed to do. I'm never this late!"

"Shit," she says again.

Shit indeed.

Three hours later, Shiva is gone, and I'm left alone with the blue and white cardboard box that will alter my life in ways I haven't yet thought of. Or maybe I have but continue to deny myself because the outcome is too uncertain. If indeed there's a baby growing inside me, it could change my relationship with Ramtin in unrecognizable ways.

Shiva insisted on staying while I took the test, but I'm not ready to know yet what the future holds. So, instead, I told her that the directions stated I take it first thing in the morning when my pee is most concentrated.

"I could be really early on and taking the test now could give me a false negative. The hormone shows up better with first pee," I explained.

"Okay, but you'd better call me as soon as you do it!" she demanded.

The truth is that I've spent the last few hours toying with the idea of being pregnant, and even though I should be terrified of having a baby out of wedlock, the number one Iranian girl sin, I'm not. Instead, I'm currently standing in front of my full-length mirror, naked, with my fingers splayed across my belly, trying to imagine what a small bulge might look like.

I hear the front door open, snapping me out of my thoughts. I suddenly regret that I decided to give Ramtin a key. Dread floods my veins like ice water, making it hard to breathe. I'm not ready to deal with him yet.

I turn on the shower and lock the bathroom door. I stare at my skin, stretched tight across my stomach, and reprimand the tears filling my eyes. If I'm pregnant, I know Ramtin won't want this baby. But I also know that I do.

Ten minutes later, I find him in the kitchen emptying bags of Indian food onto the island.

"Hey, *eshgham*," he says, leaning in to kiss me. He trails his lips across the tender skin beneath my ear, inhaling the scent of me. "You smell so good."

My body responds as it always does, tingles breaking out across the surface of my flesh. But worry weighs me down, lead woven through my legs, making the short walk to the kitchen table damn near impossible. I didn't bother to do my makeup, the nerves making my hands too shaky to apply mascara. Plus, the nausea has only worsened since this morning, and the smell of curry makes me want to gag. *It could still be food poisoning.*

Ramtin takes the seat across from me, oblivious to my current disposition.

"I'm starving," he declares.

He pulls open the lid and the smell of food gets stronger. My stomach roils again, this time forcing me to grab the table to steady myself.

"What's wrong?" he asks.

"I'm fine."

"Are you sure? You look a little yellow."

"I'm fine," I insist. "I'm just not wearing makeup." The tone in my voice leaves little room to guess at my irritation.

"Okay." He clears his throat, aggravated at my misplaced outburst. It only fuels my intolerable mood further.

He goes about the business of spooning food onto his plate, taking a big bite while watching the neighborhood kids gather their things for the night. His blatant neglect of my current state is infuriating. I push my seat away from the table, causing it to ram into the wall behind me. More dramatic of an exit than I was going for, but I fly with it, huffing as I make my way over to the bedroom.

The rational portion of my brain knows this is unnecessary, that I'm only making guesses. I don't know if I'm pregnant, and I sure as hell have no clear idea how Ramtin will react if I am. But the irrational, crazy Bita has taken over, assuming that this won't end well. And it's making me ridiculously angry.

I hear his footsteps down the hallway. I knew he would follow me—as a matter of fact, I wanted him to. Crazy Bita is itching for a fight, and it's becoming abundantly clear she won't stop until she gets one. The rational voice in my head is cautioning me to slow down, but the she-devil on my shoulder is silencing her. There's no getting off this fury train now. Rational Bita should run and hide until this is all over.

"What is going on?" Ramtin asks, leaning against the doorway. His soft, considerate tone makes me want to gag again, but this time because his understanding is sickening. I'm being a full-fledged bitch and would really appreciate the same in return. It's not a fair fight if I'm the only one in battle mode.

I just roll my eyes.

He takes a step inside, making his way over to the bed. "What's wrong?"

"You're wrong." *What does that even mean?*

"What?" The wide-eyed expression he wears confirms my behavior is shocking.

"What the hell does that mean?"

"Ugh!" I groan. Words have officially escaped me. I've morphed into an animal responding in grunts and grumbles.

Ramtin just stares at me in silence, as his eyebrows pinch into a scowl and his lips turn down in disappointment. "What is wrong with you?" he demands again. Understanding is replaced by his own ball of anger. It almost causes me to break out in a smile. *I really am crazy.*

"I'm just pissed that we've ended up here, okay?" I say.

"What? You're not making any damn sense!" *He's right; I'm not.* "I barely got here. There's no way in the last ten minutes I've done anything to get this reaction out of you."

"It's not what you did," I reply. I'm being too cryptic, but the words swirl around in my head at lightspeed and are lost on my tongue. Fear collides with anger, splashing crimson across my eyes, blurring my vision.

"You know what?" Ramtin announces, standing up. "When you want to act like a grownup, Bita, we can talk. But this is bullshit. You aren't making sense, and I haven't done anything to deserve this."

He heads toward the bedroom door, mumbling incoherently beneath his breath. I've officially pissed him off, and for some odd reason, I find it comforting.

"Call me later," he adds, over his shoulder.

As his footsteps quiet the further he gets down the hall, another wave of nausea knocks me over. This time I run to the bathroom, making it with only seconds to spare. As I heave the contents of the day into the toilet, I feel a big warm hand pull my hair back. He rubs gently in circles as he whispers words of comfort in my ear. Tears sting the back of my eyelids.

I pull abruptly away from him and lean against the wall, wiping my mouth, unladylike, with the back of my hand. His arm snaps back as the creases in his eyelids deepen. At this point, if I were him, I'd be contemplating committing me.

"I might be pregnant," I blurt out.

His expression slackens and his eyes widen at the admission. I've rendered him speechless, as he watches me rinse out my mouth and push past him back into the bedroom. My body is about to explode with nervous energy, so I begin organizing the jewelry I have scattered across my dresser, like it's the most important task at the moment. I need something to focus on other than the man staring dumbfoundedly at me from the bathroom doorway.

After what feels like an eternity, Ramtin speaks. "Will you stop for a minute?"

I drop the earrings I'm holding and turn a defiant gaze toward him. I build a fictional wall around myself, brick by brick, as a shield for what comes next. It's futile, my heart already ramming against my ribcage with such force it knocks the breath out of my lungs. I'm hovering on a cliff, unsure if Ramtin's next few words will push me over the edge, or if I'll just jump on my own volition.

"How is this possible?"

"Are you seriously going to need me to explain to you where babies come from?"

"Don't be a smartass, Bita. This is serious."

No shit. "If you're asking me if I did this on purpose, I didn't."

"I'm not saying that," he clarifies. "But we've been using protection."

"I know. I've been there."

"Would you stop!" His voice takes on the authoritative tone he uses when his daughters are giving him a hard time. The defiant teenager that lives within my chest cavity meets him head on.

"What do you want me to say?" I demand. "I'm late. That's all I know."

"Have you taken a test?"

"No."

"Then we don't know anything yet," he says, more to himself than me. "Why haven't you taken one?"

Because I've been scared. Because I don't want to know how you'll react if I am. Because I've realized that I want a baby, even if there isn't a baby now. "I didn't even notice I was late until this morning," I answer, because what I'm actually thinking makes me feel vulnerable.

Judging from the way his body is poised in fight-or-flight mode, Ramtin regards this situation as a state of emergency. The heartbreak he will render at the end of this conversation seems undeniable.

"Well, let's go get a test," he proposes, launching into motion.

"No!" He turns and looks at me, confused. "I'm supposed to take it first thing in the morning." My lame excuse to prolong the inevitable. *What is wrong with me? Why don't I want to know?* I'm not sure what scares me more, if there is a baby or there isn't.

"Okay, then, let's go get one so you can do it in the morning when we wake up."

I don't tell him that under my sink sits a brown paper bag with a pregnancy test just waiting to be taken.

"Wait." He stops, pausing for me to continue. I force the words past the sandpaper that has officially claimed my throat. "What if I am?"

"Let's hope you're not." He delivers the blow like it's nothing, having no clue that something whole is shattering inside me.

"What the hell does that mean?" Rage burns my senses in response to Ramtin's expression. *There's that stupid look again. Confused and disoriented.* "Is it that hard to believe I may actually want a baby?"

"Like this?" he asks. "We're just dating."

"Just dating? Is that what we're doing?"

"You know what I mean, Bita. We aren't even married. You want to have a baby before marriage?"

"No," I huff. "I don't know. But is that the only issue? That we aren't married?" I scrutinize. "Are you saying that if we were married you'd want a baby?" I hold my breath because despite how badly I want him to say yes, I know wishing it won't make it true.

"No," he finally answers. "I don't."

I drop my gaze to the floor, not wanting him to see the

disappointment and pain whirling inside me. My world falls apart in a few short moments, as I'm faced with a decision I've been avoiding for months. It's now or never. Either I choose to live this life with Ramtin, accepting all his limitations, or I walk away. There are no more gray lines to hide behind. He's confirmed what I've already known but was too afraid to hear.

"I don't think I can live like this."

"Like what?" I hear the hesitation in his voice, see it in the sadness claiming his eyes when I finally look at him.

"Always on the outskirts of your real life. I've given you all of me, bringing you into my world and making you a part of it. But you," I say, "just keep me in a pretty little box to open every other weekend when you don't have your kids."

"That's not true. I don't want to force you to be with us, when I know you don't always get along with my girls."

"If you really wanted a future with me, then you would keep attempting to make it work even if I get frustrated or your daughters protest. Because someday, they'd be my girls too. But you're fine living one life with me and another with your family."

"That's not fair," Ramtin protests.

He goes to continue, but I raise my hand to stop him, because I may lose my nerve if I don't say everything I need to right now. His deep, brown, desperate eyes will break my resolve and I have to rush the next words out to make sure they aren't lost in the love I feel for him.

"And I want a family of my own someday, Ramtin. I want to have a baby."

Apparently, I'm not the only one holding my breath on the outcome of this conversation as the air whooshes from between Ramtin's lips. It gives me comfort to know I'm not alone.

"I don't know what to say," he admits.

"There's nothing to say. I want babies and you don't," I state. "And this isn't going to work." I stand tall, despite feeling like I'm crumbling, as I fight the tears that have sprung to my eyes. "You should go." Ramtin flinches.

"Bita, we should talk about this," he pleads.

The anger begins to rise as bile in my throat, drowning out the fear and pain commingling in my stomach. I allow it free rein, welcome it to take over my limbs and do with me what it may, because feeling like my heart has been torn out of my chest is something I'd like to avoid.

"There isn't anything to talk about."

"But let me explain," he insists.

"Explain what?"

"My life. Babies. Everything," he answers. The agony is alight in his eyes.

"What difference will an explanation make?" I demand. Force and fury collide in each word crashing into the walls around us. I allow the crimson tide of disappointment to possess me, providing the strength I need to push forward. "You have a separate life you can't make me a part of. And you don't want kids, but I do. Sitting down for negotiations will only leave one of us disappointed in the end. Why waste any more time pretending this will work, when it so obviously won't?"

"But—"

"You should go, Ramtin."

We lock eyes, the weight of the moment pressing us down into the hardwood floor beneath our feet. I struggle to breathe, the air protesting in my lungs. But I stand my ground, knowing there is no compromise available where one of us doesn't lose.

He doesn't speak, his expression distorting with anguish when his gaze runs the length of me one last time. I can sense his apprehension, see the loss we're both feeling, reflected in the forward pull of his shoulders as he folds in on himself with regret. But I stay strong, determined not to falter. I know what I want, and I deserve to have it, even if that means losing the man I love.

Ramtin's lips take shape as if he's about to say something, but instead, he shakes his head and looks away. He turns and takes the few steps required to make it out of my bedroom and away from my aching heart. He pauses, causing the air to trap in my lungs with hope.

"Bita, I love you."

The sound of my chest heaving as my heart shatters into a million tiny pieces drowns out the shuffle of his feet and the soft click of the front door. I wrap my arms around my stomach, cradling a baby that may not even exist, as I slide to the floor. I begin to cry, for the first time allowing myself to feel the magnitude of what I've just lost.

* * *

With morning comes the smear of bright red across used toilet paper, rendering the blue and white box sitting quietly beneath my bathroom sink useless. *My luck*. I don't know whether this is good news or bad, but I stare at the folded piece of tissue for a long time. I think of Ramtin and the night before. The pain vivid in his expression and the ache throbbing in my chest. Eventually, my strength runs out, and the tears stream down my face, as I mourn a life I've spent so much time dreaming up and only minutes losing.

CHAPTER FOURTEEN

I'm sitting at my desk, staring out the window when I should be filling out charts. I've finally found five minutes of peace among the chaos of patients, and I refuse to waste them on such things as work.

My mood has progressively worsened in the past three days, each hour providing yet another outlet to sum up the list of ways Ramtin has wronged me. I don't care if he technically hasn't done anything. Crazy Bita has officially been replaced with Scorned Bita, and she's perfectly comfortable with hating him. Aside from the clarity I've acquired about my broken relationship with the first man I've ever truly loved, I've also embraced that I have multiple, and necessary, personalities living inside this vessel I refer to as a body.

The girls in the office are tiptoeing around me, trying not to wake the sleeping beast. She's not sleeping, just crouching, waiting for the attack. The worst part is, I don't really care that they're stuck dealing with my raging bitch tendencies. I know I should, but anger is the only thing keeping me sane. Behind that, there's a wall of despair I refuse to deal with. It's an all-or-nothing game right now; one false move and the house of cards will come crashing down.

A soft knock comes from the door. "Dr. Hikimi." Sandra peeks her head through the crack. "Rooms two and three are ready."

"For what?" I snap.

"Oh, sorry. For an exam and fillings."

I glare at Sandra as if she's purposely interrupted my moment of silence. "I'll be there in a minute."

I divert my gaze back to the window, setting my sights on a couple in the parking lot. He opens the door for her, she lifts up on her tiptoes to give him a kiss. They look so happy it makes my head hurt. *Stupid. It's all just a sham.*

I finally drag myself out of my seat and back into the hallway, to take care of the last few patients before my lunch break. An uninterrupted hour of peace and quiet sounds divine. I stop in front of room three, make a conscious effort to wipe the grimace off my face, replacing it with a broad, eager smile, and step inside. On days like this, I need to up my actress game. Patients don't need to experience the receiving end of my broken heart.

Four people later, my assistants are tearing down the rooms and setting up for the afternoon wave. I hurriedly make my way down the hall to my office, trying to maximize on my hour of rest. I'm halfway out of my white coat when I swing the door open to be stopped abruptly in my tracks.

"What are you doing here?"

Ramtin turns to face me. In the afternoon light, he appears to glow, flecks of stardust scattered across his skin. The gray at his temples catch the sun and look translucent against their black counterparts. The worry lines stretched across his forehead appear deeper somehow, made more obvious by the dark circles beneath his eyes. He looks his age, and it makes my lungs constrict.

The walls I've so efficiently erected around me the past few days begin to crumble to the floor, a mess of stone and rubble burying me. The heart beating uncontrollably against my ribcage is now exposed to whatever additional blows this man deems fit to render. I try to hold tightly to the anger, but it slips away as easily as water through my fingers.

"You're not taking my calls," he answers.

"I already told you I wasn't pregnant. There's nothing else to say." I pull my gown off and throw it over the back of the nearest chair, trying to focus on walking to my desk without giving away my shaking limbs. Ramtin watches me closely, a predator waiting for his prey to attempt an escape.

"But I need to talk to you, Bita," he says. The sound of my name leaving his lips is a knife to my gut. "Please, *eshgham*." And just like that, I'm bleeding out onto the office floor.

When I get the courage to meet his gaze, the tears filling his eyes crush me beneath the weight of his emotions. The knot lodged in my throat shows no mercy as it tries to burst through my flesh. Ramtin becomes a blurred image behind the sea of pain drowning my own eyes.

In an instant, I feel Ramtin's big, warm arms wrap around my waist as he pulls me into him. My face against his chest causes a rush of memories to flood my mind, one after the painful next, gutting me toward my death. The smell of his skin, swirled together with the familiar scent of his cologne, is heroin coursing through my veins. It's terrifying how badly I want to lose myself in him, in the feel of his body against mine, erasing the agony torturing me ceaselessly. It takes every ounce of strength I have to push him away, to disconnect from the one person who holds the key to my lifeline.

"Don't," I warn. "We can't do this."

"Do what? Talk?"

"Yes. I can't talk to you."

"Why not?" he asks. The desperation set in voice breaks my heart.

"Because I just can't. I need to get over you, and it's already impossible to do. Seeing you and talking to you won't help."

"I don't want you to get over me," he whispers, taking a step toward me again.

For a few brief seconds I contemplate letting him take me in his arms and make me forget all the reasons why this won't work. It would be so easy to fall back into the groove of our relationship, to push all the issues aside and pretend none of them exist. But then what good would that do? I'd be right back here again later. Maybe we'd make it a few months, or years, but he will always have another family that came before me and refuse to give me a family of my own.

"I have to."

"Bita—"

"Ramtin, please leave," I plead.

"Let me explain," he begs.

"No!"

"But I love you."

I stifle a sob before it has a chance to escape from my lips. With a shudder, I beg, "If you love me, you'll let me get over you."

He's silenced by my request. The misery in his features is so tangible I could reach out and touch it. His expression crumbles in on themselves, and his shoulders hunch forward in defeat.

"Okay, Bita. I'll go." He steps up in front of me and presses his lips against my forehead. He leans down toward my ear and whispers, "I love you."

I close my eyes and listen to his footsteps make their way out of my office and down the hall. I can't watch him go, can't see him leave me behind, despite not wanting to. I can't see that broken look in his expression again.

When I can no longer hear him, I drop my head into my hands and cry in the middle of the room, with disregard for anyone who can hear me.

* * *

Friends reruns are playing on the television, but I'm not paying much attention. I'm curled up beneath a blanket, hair up in a messy bun, still in my pajamas, despite the fact that it's a Thursday. I've called in sick because at this point, I'm convinced that a broken heart is a physical ailment. What else would explain the constant ache in my chest paired with the sudden, grief-stricken spasms in my stomach? Plus, my eyes are so red and puffy from the relentless crying and lack of sleep that I can barely see through them. Trying to do a root canal, despite the magnifying glasses I wear, would be impossible.

I hate this version of myself. This isn't who I am, this crumbled, miserable human crying on the couch. I want desperately to go back to Scorned Bita and her anger-fueled bitchiness or even Crazy Bita, who's dramatic and irrational. Anything is better than Broken Bita. But I don't have the energy necessary to pull myself out of this hole. So, instead, I've told myself I get two days. I'll fake the flu, call in sick, and curl up under this blanket for forty-eight hours. I'll allow myself all the tears and sadness my body can handle, but when Saturday morning rolls around, I'm done. That's the plan.

I'm startled awake by knocking at the door. For a moment I'm disoriented, unaware that I've fallen asleep and thrown off by the dimness of the living room. *What time is it?*

The knocking comes again, this time more aggressive. I force myself off the couch, realizing that the disturbance isn't going to the take the hint, and wrap the blanket around my shoulders as I go.

More knocking.

"Hold on! I'm coming." I swing the door open, ready to pounce on whatever annoying salesperson is awaiting me. Instead, I find Shiva.

"Shit!" she exclaims. "This is worse than I thought."

I don't respond, just muster up my best dirty look and walk back to the couch, leaving the door open for her to follow.

"You're pregnant," she concludes, taking the seat across from me. The concern on her face is annoying as hell.

"No, I'm not pregnant."

"Oh, thank God." She exhales as if she's the one who's just dodged the baby bullet. I ungracefully fall over on the couch, returning to my fetal position.

"Now that you know, can you leave me alone so I can go back to sleep?" I beg.

"Yeah, that's not happening," she says. "What the hell is wrong with you?"

"Nothing."

"Uh, your greasy hair and wrinkled pajamas say differently. And don't get me started on your puffy face."

"Leave me alone, Shiva. I don't want to talk about it." I sound like a whining child, but I can't help it. I know my best friend, and I'm fully aware she won't leave, and I'll be talking about it against my will.

"You know I'm not doing that." She gets up and turns on the lights.

"Oh, my God! Can you shut those off?" Now I know what the Wicked Witch felt like when they poured water on her head.

"Nope," she argues. "Come on." She stands in front of the couch, hand outstretched to help me up.

"Where are we going?" I ask, frustrated.

"The shower," she demands. "Then I'm ordering some food and opening a bottle of wine, and you're telling me why you look like a miserable zombie right now."

I just stare up at her, too tired to even give her a dirty look. She's tapping her foot impatiently, and I'm tempted to throw the blanket over my head until she goes away.

"Don't make me call your mom," she threatens. "Or better yet, don't make me call Maziar."

"Screw you," I huff, letting her drag me off the couch. "I hate you."

"I know," she answers, but still makes me get in the damn shower.

I spend the next ten minutes standing beneath the hot water trying to devise a distraction plan. Reliving the details, I'm failing miserably at forgetting, will not help my current mental state. But my body is heavy with defeat, and my mind is sluggish, and I can't come up with any ideas. Once I'm in a clean pair of sweats, sitting at the kitchen table with a full glass of wine in hand, and food is on its way, Shiva's finally content.

"Okay, what the hell happened?"

"We broke up," I answer. *Might as well get this over with.*

"What?" she replies. "Why?"

"It just wasn't working out."

"Oh, you know I'm going to need more than that, so spill."

I spend the next hour regurgitating the events of the past few days. I never told anyone my fears about Ramtin's lack of desire for more children, because I didn't want to give my family and friends a reason to try to talk me out of being with him. Judging from the small gasps and the furrowing of Shiva's brow, she wasn't expecting it. I make sure to describe in great detail Ramtin's less than perfect reaction to the news of a possible pregnancy, leaving little room for Shiva to feed me any hope where this relationship is concerned.

"Oh, shit."

"Yeah, shit indeed," I confirm.

"No. You don't understand," she replies, her hand flying up to cover her mouth so I can't see that her jaw has dropped open.

"What?"

"I messed up," she says.

"What did you do?" My nerves start buzzing on overdrive. I have no idea what Shiva could have done to make this already horrible situation worse, but nonetheless, I feel like puking.

"I called Kian. You told me I should call him and so I just went for it."

"Okay." I exhale. Kian and Shiva. It isn't ideal, but it's not the end of the world.

"We're supposed to go out Saturday night," she admits. "If you want, I'll cancel it."

"No, it's fine."

I don't know if seeing Shiva with Kian will be as difficult as it feels, but I know she likes him. I don't have the heart to ruin something that could potentially be amazing for her, just because I'm selfish. I rolled the dice and lost. She shouldn't have to pay for it.

"Are you sure?" I can hear the hopefulness in her voice.

"Yes. Go and have a good time," I insist.

"I'll make sure he knows what a jerk his brother is," she adds.

"Okay," I say, laughing for the first time in days.

CHAPTER FIFTEEN

"Hello?" I call. "Mom?"

"In the kitchen," she yells back.

The melodic familiarity in my mother's tone and the smells of Shabbat dinner swirl together to create a blanket of comfort I pull in around my shoulders as I make my way farther inside. This is the first Friday night dinner since Ramtin and I broke up that I couldn't give a lame excuse to get out of. Working late and a splitting headache will only go so far before the cavalry is sent to check in on my whereabouts.

"Hi, *azizam*," Mom says as I wrap my arms around her waist and bury my head in the crook of her neck like a small child. She kisses the top of my crown, her hands occupied with plating chicken and *gondee. Meatballs mixed with garbanzo beans.* She glances above me before adding, "Where's Ramtin?"

Ramtin has come to a few Shabbat dinners, and now Mom thinks that means he's joining every week. Guess she didn't get the memo that we currently hate him.

"He's not coming," I answer, still cuddling her. I refuse to look up and see the concern etched into her features. I don't need to see her expression to sense the energy shift around her.

Suddenly, a heavy, calloused hand runs gently across my head, as Dad kisses my temple. I didn't even hear him come in, with his stealthy ninja skills.

I inhale, feeling Mom's body tense beneath my fingertips. I ready myself for the barrage of questions that are about to follow, when the sound of the front door interrupts the looming interrogation.

"Hi," Maziar and Sara chirp in unison, making their way into the kitchen.

We take a few minutes to dish out kisses and give each other love, like the proper Persian family we are. Then Sara immediately jumps into helping Mom with the dinner prep. I take her lead, busying myself with spooning white rice onto a platter, on the opposite side of the kitchen.

Once the mound is even, I fill a separate bowl with more rice and pour the dissolved *zafaran, saffron,* on top, mixing until it's all a golden yellow. I proceed to use it to create symmetrical lines across the platter, designing a checkerboard appearance. Next, I grab the fried *keshmesh, raisins,* off the stove and fabricate a swirling pattern on top of the multicolored rice. In about ten minutes, my masterpiece will end up a jumbled mess of food, but for now, I'm hoping my attempt to dazzle Mom with my amazing Iranian hostess skills is enough to distract her from Ramtin's absence. Sadly, no dice.

"Where did you say Ramtin was tonight?" she suddenly asks. Mom sends me a sidelong glance, her gaze still steady on the dish in front of her. There's no mistaking she's feeling me out, trying to decipher whether I'm about to feed her a lie.

"I didn't," I answer. "He's just not coming." I send a silent prayer she drops it. Long shot; this woman can break the best of them.

Maziar is eyeing me, as he leans on the kitchen counter beside her. We lock eyes and I desperately beg him telepathically to leave it alone. He raises a brow, but when I don't offer up any further information, he gets the hint.

"Mom, did I tell you they're discussing making me a senior associate at the firm?" he says. "It's a big deal, since I've only been there for a few years. But they're really happy with my performance." *A diversion. My brother is brilliant sometimes.*

Mom sends me one last glance, then lets the Ramtin issue rest for the moment, moving onto my brother's good news. "*Afareen, pesaram. Bravo, my son,*" she replies. "What does that mean, exactly? Will your workload increase?"

"Yes, but so will my pay." The youthful giddiness that consumes him makes me giggle. He squeezes my hand as he grabs the platter of rice I've just finished decorating. "Mom, look. Bita listens when you try to teach her how to be a good Persian wife," he teases, showing off my artistic design.

"That's nice, *azizam,*" she says. The smile she gives me isn't as brilliant as usual; she's having trouble hiding her concern.

I grab the dish of chicken she's finished, kiss her cheek, and escape to the dining room, trying to ignore the roiling apprehension in my stomach.

Fifteen minutes later, we're seated, prayers have been said, and food is being passed around. Mom watches me from across the table, quietly waiting on my confession. It has almost been a month, but the thought of Ramtin still causes a lump to form in my throat. It suffocates me with all that I've loved and lost.

I'm not over him, despite wanting desperately to be. But I'm not spending every night crying either. *That's progress, right?* I'm focused and slowly working toward putting back the pieces of my broken heart. But for some reason, telling my family that we're through makes me physically ill. Maybe it's the disappointment I'll witness in their faces, or maybe saying it out loud to my parents somehow makes it final.

Mom gently lays her fork and spoon on the edge of her dish and leans forward in her seat, resting her chin on her intertwined fingers. *Oh, shit. It's go time.*

"Where's Ramtin?" Mom asks. Her tone is eerily even and calm, causing everyone at the table to quiet in their seats.

"At home, I'd guess."

"Why is he at home?" Mom huffs, obviously not amused by my attempt at evading her questions.

I take a deep breath, exhaling slowly as I try to stall. My mind is racing, deciding if I tell the truth or feed them a lie. How long can I keep this charade up before it becomes painstakingly obvious that we're no longer together? A few weeks? Another month? My parents aren't idiots.

It most definitely would be horrible if they heard it from someone else. I can say with certainty that Ramtin won't go around running his mouth, but there's a good chance Roya will. My gut tells me she'll not only spread rumors about me but will enjoy it. It will be a matter of time before someone whispers my secret into Mom's ear. At that point, who knows what the game of telephone will have conceived?

"We broke up." My silent audience stills even further. Sara sinks back into her seat, pity and despair etched into her features. I hate that look. I've been getting it for weeks from my friends. "It's a good thing," I insist.

"Why is that?" Dad asks.

"Because we just want different things."

"Like?" Mom probes.

"Guys, I don't really want to talk about it. Just trust me. It wasn't going to work out."

"Are you sure you weren't just being dramatic?" Mom questions. "You know, you have a tendency to blow things out of proportion."

I try not to react to Mom's blatant reference to Crazy Bita. I have become quite fond of the parts of me that are less than appealing to my family.

"I'm not overreacting, Mom. Give me some credit. I'm not a child."

I spoon a heaping mound of rice onto my plate and shovel it into my mouth with charisma. Judging from Mom's wide-eyed expression, I've successfully pulled her attention to the carb loading I'm currently taking in. Iranian women watch their figures; carbs are the devil. Obviously, neither applies to me now. *The perfect distraction.*

* * *

"What are you guys doing here?" I ask. Maziar and Sara are sitting on my porch.

"Waiting for you, silly," Sara answers.

"I can see that," I reply, unlocking the front door. "Did we have plans?" I scroll through my mind but come up blank. I don't remember committing to anything. Surely they would have reminded me last night at dinner.

"Nope." Sara weaves her arm through mine as we step inside. "We wanted to take you out to lunch."

"Really, guys. I'm fine." I pull myself out of Sara's hold, suddenly feeling the need to have a plan of escape if they start asking questions. Her grasp on me will make it difficult to hide in the bathroom. "You don't need to cheer me up or anything."

"Of course you're fine," Maziar encourages. "You're my badass sister. No one gets the best of you. Other than me." He winks.

"Ha, ha. Funny."

"We just wanted to hang out with you, that's all," Maziar adds. "Wait, why are you so sweaty? Did you just come from the gym?" He scans my outfit, taking in the leggings and sports bra.

"Oh, no," I answer. "I'm avoiding the gym. You know, running into the ex and all. I just went for a run."

"Well we can wait. Go shower, because I'm going to lose my appetite if I have to deal with your stink all day," he teases. I playfully punch him in the arm before heading to my room.

Ten minutes later, I find them sprawled out on my couch, channel surfing. "Make yourselves at home," I say, feigning irritation.

Maziar flashes me a broad grin. "You ready?"

We decide on our usual café, due to its proximity. I'd like to make this torture as short-lived as possible. If Sara looks at me again with that damn pity in her eyes, I may punch her. And Maziar constantly alluding to how awesome and strong I am. As if I don't realize he's trying to boost my confidence. Well, my confidence is just fine! And they're both annoying the hell out of me.

I know their hearts are in the right place, though, so I try to brighten up my mood and will myself to engage in mundane conversation. I laugh and nod at all the right places, ask all the right questions, and pretend that my life didn't implode four weeks ago. I try to keep us talking because awkward silences will just give them an opening to ask me questions. I don't want to talk about me. Or Ramtin.

Maziar holds the door open as Sara and I squeeze through side-by-side, giggling at our horrible coordination. I'm starting to ease into the afternoon, shedding the tension gripping my shoulders, when I almost barrel into someone.

"Oh, sorry," I apologize, before I've seen who it is.

"Bita?" Kimiya's childlike voice startles me.

"Hi," I sputter. "What are you doing here?"

"We came to have lunch," she answers. She looks at Maziar and Sara, giving them a small wave. "Hi."

"Guys, this is Kimiya. Ramtin's daughter."

"Hey," Sara says, before there's a chance for things to get awkward.

As she carries on a conversation with Kimiya, I try to scan the room looking for her adult companion. Part of me wishes it's Ramtin, the other dreads that it may be. When Roya steps up beside her, I realize she's the worse of the options.

"Hello, Bita *joon*." Her sickly-sweet tone makes me want to gag. *Who does this bitch think she's fooling?*

"Hi, Roya." I try hard to suppress Bitchy Bita from blatantly painting her disdain across the café walls.

She glances over my shoulder at Maziar. "Is this your brother?" she asks. The flirtatious energy beaming off her has me wanting to slap her even more. As if my hot, younger brother would give her the time of day!

"Yes, he is, and I'm Sara." Roya startles as if she's just noticed my sister-in-law standing beside Maziar. Sara wraps her arms protectively around her husband and adds, "His wife." She glares at Roya's rude disregard for her, while Maziar stands there grinning ridiculously.

"Well," she says. "*Khoshbakhtam. Pleasure to meet you.*" She takes hold of Kimiya's hand. "We have to get going. Come on, Kimiya. Your dad is waiting." She makes sure to send me a knowing glance at the mention of Ramtin. "Family lunch plans," she adds. The smirk pulled across her injected lips causes me to almost take a step forward. Bitchy Bita is ready to throw punches.

Sara's hand suddenly rests on my shoulder, her grip tight enough to give me pause. Kimiya's innocent eyes staring up at me have me counting ten, trying to calm down. It's not this poor girl's fault her mom's a jerk. She doesn't deserve to be stuck in our silent feud.

"Will you be coming by soon?" Kimiya asks. I can see the hope nestled in her young pupils. *She knows.*

Before I have a chance to reply, Roya does it for me. "No, *azizam*, I don't think so. Daddy and Bita aren't close friends anymore. Remember, Daddy told you that."

"Yeah, I remember." Kimiya's face closes off with disappointment and my chest begins to ache. I knew she liked me, but I never thought that my disappearance would have this kind of effect on her. When she tries to hide her feelings behind a smile, it breaks my heart further.

"Let's go," Roya commands. "Nice meeting you all." She winks at Maziar, and Sara's nostrils flair with aggravation.

"Wish we could say the same thing," Sara mumbles under her breath.

"Hold my earrings, Sissy, so I can meet this bitch in the parking lot," I half-tease.

"That's funny." Maziar chuckles. "But she really is a piece of work."

"Totally not worth it," Sara adds, squeezing my shoulder.

"I know," I say. "But, damn, it's nice to dream."

* * *

"Room two is ready for an exam, Doctor."

We have a new assistant. She's young and green and thoroughly terrified of me. It's pretty marvelous.

"Let's go up to the front desk, Mrs. Cohen, and we can make an appointment for your next exam." I help her out of the chair and allow her to use my arm for support as we make the short, but slow, walk to the waiting room. Her steely gray locks and rosy cheeks have me hoping I'm this put-together at her age. For ninety, she's all rainbows and sunshine.

"You should really meet my grandson," she says. I giggle at her dedication. She tries to set me up with him every time she comes in. "He's such a handsome boy, that Michael of mine. He's tall, with the unique brownish-red hair and the most piercing blue eyes."

"I know, Mrs. Cohen. You've told me about him before."

"Oh, I know dear," she replies, patting my hand. "I just figure if I keep on telling you, maybe you'll finally give in."

"He's lucky to have such a wonderful grandmother as you," I answer. "I have to go see some other patients now, but I'll see you soon, okay?" She squeezes my hand before I leave her with my front office staff.

As I walk back to room two, I daydream about how much easier it would be to take Mrs. Cohen up on her offer. Her grandson is young, established, never been married. No baggage. *That's what I need in my life.*

I grab the chart off the tray hanging on the door and flip to the patient's health history. I'm on autopilot, just looking for any concerning medical issues I should know about before we get started. What I neglect to notice is the name in bold, black letters, printed across the top.

"Hi there," I say. "I'm Doctor Hakimi, I'll be seeing you today." When I get no response, I glance over to find Yasi staring at me with her big brown eyes. They're as deep as Ramtin's, as if she carries the weight of the world in them.

I stop abruptly and am left totally speechless. Partly because I see her father, and partly because there's no way she's sitting here. *I've finally lost it.*

"Before you get mad, let me explain," she blurts out. I just blink, unable to wrap my mind around what I'm seeing. "I needed to talk to you," she continues. When I still don't say anything, she reaches out and gently touches my arm. "Are you okay, Bita?"

The feel of her warm fingertips against my skin breaks my catatonic state. "What are you doing here, Yasi?"

"I told you: I need to talk to you."

"Do your parents know you're here?" More specifically, *does Ramtin know you're here?*

"No," she admits, hanging her head and pulling at a frayed thread on her shorts.

"How did you get here?"

All I need is for Roya to find out Yasi hitchhiked over to my office. All kinds of hell would break loose. Now that I think of it, seeing the look on Roya's face, when she hears that her daughter came across town to talk to Ramtin's ex, will be insanely satisfying. I have to consciously stop the smirk that's tugging at the corner of my lip.

"I took the bus."

"You know how to take the bus?" Out of everything going on now, this bit of info shocks me the most.

"Yes," she answers. I hear a hint of her teenage attitude and I smile. Its familiarity anchors me in the chaos.

"Okay." I exhale. She isn't leaving—that much is clear—so I scoot my chair over until I'm facing her. "What's going on?"

She carefully raises her head until her gaze meets mine. Whatever she sees eases the tension out of her coiled muscles.

"You have to take my dad back."

I almost choke on my own spit. "What?" Now I know I must be having a nervous breakdown, because I'm hallucinating. Either that, or I'm stuck in some strange twilight zone. First Kimiya's heartfelt run-in and now this.

"He's miserable without you, Bita. He hasn't been the same since you guys broke up." The silent desperation in her expression is beyond her years. She's too young to understand all the intricacies that are woven into the fibers of a relationship, that each thread can be another obstacle to unravel it all. But despite her lack of life experience, the pleading in her voice gives me pause.

"Yasi, it's not that easy," I explain.

"Look, Bita, I'm not a child. I understand that it's complicated." Her expression hardens at the insult I wasn't meaning to give.

"I'm sorry. I know you aren't a little kid." I reach out and squeeze her hand, her eyes softening in return.

"I don't mean to be a bitch," she says.

"Did you just say that?" I laugh. "Are you allowed to use that word?"

"No," she responds. Her sheepish grin and flushed cheeks cause a warmth to stir in my chest. "But I mean it. I don't try to be difficult. Sometimes I can't help it."

"I'm pretty sure that's your job at this age. Being difficult," I tease.

"If that's one of the reasons why you can't be with my dad, I promise I'll do better."

Her face is somber, regret twisting up in a knot of apprehension, causing the words to be lost in my throat. The remorse she harbors only cracks my broken heart further.

"It has nothing to do with you," I insist. "You and I are okay." I don't know if she believes me; the determination in her eyes giving nothing away.

She exhales, long and deep, as if she's been holding her breath for a lifetime. "But Bita, I'm serious, you guys have to get back together." She can't keep the pleading out of her voice.

"Has he said something to you?"

"No. He won't talk to us about that stuff. Not because we're kids," she clarifies, "but he doesn't want us to worry or feel bad for him. I can see it, though. He's really sad without you."

I lean back in my chair, the weight of this young girl's world pressing me into the seat. The breath rushing in and out of my lungs is labored with the disappointment I'm about to deliver. How do I explain to Yasi that her dad and I are just on different paths, ones we can't merge? How do I break this girl's heart as her fierce gaze makes me question my choices?

"Please, Bita. Just talk to him," she begs.

I'm amazed at how many layers and how much depth I'm discovering in Yasi. I don't remember being this brave at fifteen. "I'll think about it, okay?" It's all I can promise her.

"Okay," she says. The little glimmer of hope causes her face to shine. Despite not being what she wanted to hear, I can sense her relief. "Thanks."

"You're welcome." The warmth pumping through my heart is surprising. I never would have guessed that just a few months after my first encounter with the little she-devil, we'd find ourselves friends. "Now, where are you supposed to be?" I ask.

"My dad's," she groans. "I can just hop back on the bus and head home. You don't have to worry about it." It's apparent in her wide-eyed expression that she hadn't thought her plan through. At least not to the point where she'd be receiving some consequences for not letting anyone know about her afterschool detour.

"Yeah, that's not happening," I reply. "You know I'm going to have to call your dad, right?" At the mention of Ramtin, she suppresses a small lip twitch. *Maybe she did think this through? That sneaky little genius.* I have to hold back my own chuckle of admiration. For a fifteen-year-old, she sure is cunning.

"No, don't do that," she answers, trying her best to be Oscar-worthy.

"Oh, save it." She can't hold back her grin. "You really are something, Yasi," I tease.

"I try."

I make the short walk back to my office so I can call Ramtin in private. Despite it being part of Yasi's master plan, I don't want her to witness the million nerves firing off in trepidation as I speak to the man I love, for the first time in what feels like a lifetime.

My fingers shake as I dial his number, and I curse myself for not being the stone-cold badass I wish I were.

"Bita?" Ramtin answers on the first ring.

"Hi, Ramtin." I have to focus on keeping the quiver out of my voice, but the rolling waves in my belly are not making it easy.

"How are you?" The yearning embedded in his words flashes like headlights across the phone lines.

I can feel the walls erected around me bend and pull in his direction. I have to force myself to stay on task. "Yasi is here in my office."

"Yasi is there?" The news is as shocking to him as it was when I first walked into my operatory to find her.

"Yes. She came here after school to talk to me."

"What the hell? About what?"

"About us," I answer, willing my voice not to crack. The knot set squarely in my throat is currently making it impossible to speak. *Get your shit together, Bita.*

"Oh." He pauses, exhaling loudly. "This girl is going to be the end of me," he mumbles to himself. "I'm so sorry she disrupted your day, Bita. I had no idea she would do this." His tone is suddenly back to business, and it stings. "How did she even get there? Please tell me she didn't hitchhike!"

"No, she took the bus." The similarity in our thoughts should be comforting but it's not.

"She knows how to take the bus?" Again, being on the same page with Ramtin is depressing. It's confirmation that we're an amazing pair, but thanks to time and the past, we can't be together.

"I didn't want you guys to be worried." I push forward. "I know she was supposed to be home a few hours ago." *Stay focused, Bita. This isn't a friendly call. You aren't with this man anymore.* "I still have patients, but I can drop her off if you want me to. She'd have to hang out in my office for a few hours, though. I can't get away right now."

"No. She's already inconvenienced your day enough. Is it okay if I swing by and pick her up?" I can hear his hesitation.

"Sure." *It'll be fine; I'll just send her outside to meet him, and I won't have to deal with the awkward interaction.* Even as I think it, I know there's no way he's showing up to my work and I'm going to pass up the chance to see him.

There's nothing more I want then to take in the deep set of his brown eyes, feeling their gaze settle on my skin, as he sets my nerves on fire by just existing. The sharp outline of his jaw, feeding into his plump, kissable lips, make all my good parts pound in anticipation. In this moment, I want nothing more than to be in the same space as he is. And it's terrifying.

"Okay. I'm just finishing up. I can be there in about fifteen."

"Sounds good." My tone is grossly chipper; I almost make myself gag.

"Thanks, Bita," he replies. "I appreciate you calling me."

"No problem. See you in a few."

I settle Yasi in my office and run off to attend to the next patient. Despite knowing I shouldn't see Ramtin, I can't help but rush through my exam, constantly glancing at the clock to make sure I complete it in the fifteen-minute window. When I make my way back to my office, Yasi is gone.

My stomach drops at the loss of a chance to see Ramtin again. I'm fighting tears when I hear Yasi's shuffle behind me. I whip around to see her standing in my doorway, looking down at her phone.

"He's here," she announces, not aware that I'm mid-heart attack. She lifts her gaze to meet mine and asks, "Will you walk me out?"

Say no. Say no. "Yes." *Stupid!* A grin stretches across Yasi's face, while I'm buried beneath a mountain of uneasiness.

My legs move on their own volition, following her down the hall and out the front door, the load of my staff's curiosity boring holes into my back. No one asks where I'm going, silently watching through the front windows. I can hear the rumor mill churning already, but I don't care, my sights set on the most amazing man I've ever seen.

Ramtin steps out of his car, his lean frame skinnier since the last time I saw him. He looks tired, dark circles invading the thin skin beneath his eyes, but his stare is intense and determined. Its purity is filled with longing and regret. I can hardly breathe when he steps up to me, so close I can see the small details of his scar.

"Bye, Bita," Yasi calls over her shoulder, scrambling into the car to give us privacy. At this point, she could be standing beside me and I wouldn't notice. The only thing I can see is Ramtin.

"Hi," he whispers. His voice punctures my heart with its familiarity.

"Hi."

He pauses, taking in the contour of my face. I feel exposed and raw beneath his penetrating awareness. My body hums with his proximity, and I have to consciously root my feet to the ground so I don't lean into his arms and out of my common sense. I want so badly to lose myself again, to be with this beautiful man, to convince myself that he's enough. But the truth is that he's not. I want more, and he can't give it to me. Or rather, he won't.

"How are you?"

It takes me a moment to reel it all in, but I do, taking on the businesslike tone I need to make it through this conversation. "I'm good, thanks. But I really need to get back. I have a few patients waiting for me."

I see the disappointment cross his expression, but Ramtin is too much of a proud Iranian man to let it get the best of him. "Of course," he says. His compliance is another punch to the gut. "I won't keep you. Thanks again for humoring Yasi. I'll make sure this doesn't happen again." With that, he reaches out and squeezes my arm in a friendly, platonic fashion, suffocating my demolished heart.

"No problem." My tone is clipped and tight. "Have a good day."

"You, too."

He's already making his way over to the driver side of his car. I spin on my heels and head back into the office. My staff stares as I stomp past them, aware that the bear is officially awake and that no one wants to mess with her today. I slam my door and wince. *Shit, I hope that wasn't too loud.* I hold my breath, waiting for my boss to storm in and fire me for my erratic behavior. I wouldn't blame him; I've been a certifiable nut case lately. When no footsteps come, I exhale. *I need to get it together.*

I step over to the window and notice that Ramtin's car is still sitting idly in front of the building. I'm not sure what he's doing, but I can see Yasi's arms flailing around as she passionately says something to her father. I can't help but imagine her telling him off for being such a moron for losing me. The thought makes me smile, despite the cruel ache in my chest. When his car finally pulls away, tears sting the back of my eyes.

Every time I say goodbye to Ramtin, it hurts. My world crumbles around me and the devastation left behind traps me in despair. Is this all worth it? Is there no way back from here? A baby. Is that what it would take? How badly do I need a child of my own?

Things have shaped up considerably with his daughters. Kimiya's longing gaze and Yasi's fierce determination haunt me. My gut tells me those relationships can evolve into something beautiful. Maybe loving his daughters would be enough. The problem is I'm so tangled in the web of wants and desires versus needs and common sense that I can't see straight anymore.

The pain pounding in my heart is rapidly progressing toward a flat line. My breath is ragged with panic and my fingers tingle with desperation. There's an imaginary clock ticking away in my mind, the hands flying by as I run out of precious time.

This morning, I knew what I wanted, and I was willing to accept what it would cost me. But now, I'm not so sure.

CHAPTER SIXTEEN

I stir my drink with the thin black straw, listening to the melodic clinking of the ice cubes as they hit the glass. I'm leaning against the table, watching Kian ordering around the restaurant staff while Shiva stands a few feet away from him, staring in admiration. Even from this distance, I can see how she feels about him. It's bouncing off the walls like a rubber ball. If this were a cartoon, there'd be hearts in a dreamy bubble above her head. He stops every few demands, leans in and gently kisses her lips, her temple, the tip of her nose. It's adorable and heartbreaking, all at the same time.

I showed up an hour early, thinking I could be useful setting up. But it's painfully apparent I'm not needed. The pit of jealousy that sits firmly in my stomach is spreading like an unwanted disease, despite my best efforts to stop it. I'm over the moon for my best friend; I really am. She deserves this happiness, her first go at real love. And Kian is a great guy, from what she tells me, anyway. I've been so preoccupied with shooting my own love life to hell that there's been little time to mingle with her new love interest. I regret it now, as I stand on the outskirts of their relationship like an impostor, glued to their public display of affection as I sulk over the loss of my own.

When Kian finally has the staff adhering to his birthday bash guidelines, he grabs Shiva's hand and spins her in the middle of the restaurant, pulling her body to his and dipping her toward the ground, planting a sensual kiss on her lips as her cheeks become rosy with glee. I have to look away, feeling like an intruder on a very intimate moment.

I return my gaze to my glass, the ice cubes almost completely melted, watering down my vodka tonic. *Sad. But easier to down.* I toss back the contents in one big gulp. It burns my throat and I eagerly await the aftereffects. I'm going to need a nice, warm buzz if I'm making it through tonight. With Shiva's ridiculous guest list, there will be a lot of socializing and mingling I'm not interested in, nor have the energy for. Hence alcohol, to blur the edges and speed up time, will be my salvation.

As the waiter comes by to pick up my now-empty glass, I ask for another. There's a crowd forming at the entrance, the guests making their way into the party in quick succession. Shiva set the time on the invite for an hour earlier than the party was to start, taking "Persian time" into consideration. *Pretty smart.* Fashionably late is an accessory Iranians wear like a pair of pretty bangles.

The music is vibrating off the walls, causing a pounding in my aching head. *Or is it my aching heart, radiating toward my brain?* It's hard to tell. Each touch Kian places on Shiva's hip or on the small of her back is another reminder of how I picked the wrong brother. I wince at my own thoughts, realizing I'm truly such a bitch. *Wrong brother? That's just spiteful.*

"Ugh," I grumble, pushing the voice of reason as far into the dark crevices of my mind as possible. I have no interest in being nice. Not at the moment, anyway. Mean, angry, unyielding, those are the adjectives I'm going for.

"Hey, Bita." Pouyah's voice sounds smooth and seductive, causing the hairs to stand on the back of my neck.

I turn to find curious gray eyes staring at me. "Hi, Pouyah."

"How are you?" he asks. The gentility in his voice is irritating. And the pity in his scrunched lids is infuriating. The fact that he knows my heart's been broken in two makes me want to punch him. I don't want him to know anything about me, and I sure as hell don't need his concern.

"I'm doing just fine," I answer. I hope he picks up on the smugness in my voice.

"That's good," he says. "Just wanted to check."

"And why is that?" I can't help myself as I challenge him. *What is wrong with me?* Complacency would have had this conversation done and over with.

"I'm sorry; what?" He looks confused.

If I didn't know him, I'd think he cared. But I do know him, and I don't care if he cares. I'm pissed he'd have the audacity to think I needed his kindness. *You've lost your mind,* Rational Bita says. *Just shut up,* I throw back at her. Maybe I have gone crazy.

"Uhm, I just wanted to know how you were doing, that's all."

"Yeah, I bet."

"I don't know what your deal is, Bita, but you're acting strange."

"Strange? Or bitchy?" I raise a brow, daring him to say it.

"Like I said, I was just checking in," he answers, brushing off my advances toward an argument. He shakes his head. "I'm going to go." With that he turns and walks away, getting swallowed in the impressive crowd. *Damn shame. I would have rather enjoyed that fight.*

I turn back to the refilled drink sitting before me. The waiter must have dropped it on the table and run. *He didn't deserve that,* Rational Bita says.

"Oh shut up," I mumble. *Great! I'm talking to myself. Like out loud! I should probably call Maziar for a ride to the asylum right about now.* Instead, I take another long sip of the godly elixir sitting in front of me. I welcome the medicinal tang that bursts across my taste buds.

"Hey." Kian startles me out of my thoughts.

"Oh. Hey."

"You doing okay over here?"

"Why does everyone keep asking me if I'm okay?" I blurt out. Okay, so not everyone, but still. Being asked the same question within a five-minute time span is unnerving. Am I that transparent?

"Well," Kian replies, leaning his elbows on the pub table I've claimed as my own. Judging from the wide berth the crowd is making, they know not to attempt to claim the three quarters of its surface still available. "If your scowl, and the way you're about to shatter the glass grasped between your fingers, is any indication, I'd say you are definitely giving off a 'leave me the hell alone' vibe."

I straighten up, suddenly aware of the tension in my shoulders, and the unflattering pull of my brow. Kian chuckles at my futile attempt at appearing like I'm not in the worst of moods. I don't even really know what my problems is. Nothing has happened to elicit such bitter fueled expressions, but tonight, I'm back at the anger phase in the seven stages of grief.

Kian's sudden appearance isn't making it any easier. The sadness that tugs at my chest, when I notice how the curve of his nose and the sharp angle of his jaw are identical to his older brother's, stops the air from passing through my lungs. It's an unwelcome reminder of how much I miss Ramtin.

The tears threatening to fill my eyes force me to avert my gaze, as I pray I don't start bawling in the middle of my best friend's birthday party while my ex's brother is watching. That would be beyond humiliating. I try to shake it off, hiding my emotions behind a ridiculously wide smile.

"Are you having a good time?" I ask. Change the subject; move the focus off me and onto him. My current go-to plan these days.

"Yeah," he answers. The kindness in his soft brown irises makes it harder to fight the knot lodged in my throat. "Shiva seems to be enjoying herself."

We both glance over in her direction, watching her whirl around on the dance floor with Parisa, drink spilling carelessly onto the floor.

"She is," I reply. "Thanks for doing all of this for her. It's really sweet of you. She's lucky to have you."

"I'm the lucky one."

I tip my head to the side and take another sip of my drink, sizing him up as he stares at his girlfriend. Kian says all the right things, but as I watch him watching Shiva, I have no doubt he genuinely means it.

My despondency morphs into a cinder block, forcing me beneath the waves. There's not enough alcohol in the world to drown out this pain. I look down at my empty glass and push it away from me. No point to keep going.

"So," Kian says, returning his attention back to me. "How are you?"

He's obviously not letting this go. And the piercing intensity of his eyes confirm that he's not looking for the details of my day. Honestly, I'm too tired to fake it any longer. It's hard putting up a front all the time, only admitting my broken heart to myself in the dark hours of the early morning.

"I'm not sure," I answer. "Some days I'm fine. Others," I say pointing to my empty glass, "I'm not."

"I can get that," Kian acknowledges. "Why don't you talk to Ramtin?"

"Because what would be the point?"

"The difference between anger and understanding."

"Do you even know why we broke up?" I question, suddenly irritated again.

"Look," he says, raising his hands in apology. "I don't mean to overstep."

"No, I'm sorry." I sigh. "I'm such a bitch all the time lately. I'm not trying to be." I rub my hand across my face, trying to wipe away my moodiness.

"It's cool." He reaches out and squeezes my hand. "We've all been there." His concerned expression is so familiar it stabs me in the heart. "But things aren't always black and white, Bita," he continues, completely oblivious that his mere resemblance to his brother is causing me to bleed out onto the floor. "Sometimes there's an explanation that brings you to a gray area you didn't see before. It's the difference between losing a relationship or healing it."

"I don't think there's a gray area here." I can't keep the hopelessness out of my voice.

"He may surprise you." Kian glances over my shoulder at something. "Give him a chance."

"Bita?" His voice causes my heart to stop mid-beat.

"Don't hate me," Kian begs, squeezing my hand one more time, then turning to leave.

"Bita," he says again. He's closer now. I can feel the heat radiating off his body, feel his breath flutter across the back of my neck. The smell of his cologne at this proximity is intoxicating. As it fills my lungs, the love I feel for him pushes against my restraints.

I can't do this alone.

He lightly touches my shoulder and I almost lose myself. The sparks shooting down my arm at the mere feel of his fingertips is evidence that I won't make it through this conversation whole. Not that I'm in one piece now. Half of me is living inside the man standing behind me. He's claimed the deepest parts of me, and I don't think I'll ever get them back.

I see Kian and Shiva watching us from the corner. The apology set in Shiva's worried lips would normally make me angry, but at the moment, all I can feel is my heart trying to rip through my ribcage.

I slowly turn, holding my breath, worried I may have dreamed Ramtin out of thin air. But when I see those brooding dark eyes staring down at me, I realize it's not my imagination. He's really here, and it's utterly devastating.

"Can we talk?"

I can't find words, lost between my heart and mouth. I watch him pull his lip between his teeth in apprehension and I've never wanted to lean in and kiss him more. When his hand reaches up and gently rests on my cheek, I can't stop myself from leaning into it, tears threatening to blur my vision.

He takes another step toward me, his chest lightly brushing against mine with each breath I take. When I look up into his longing gaze, I can sense my body gravitating toward him, feel the kiss forming on my lips before I've even made the decision to kiss him. I force myself to take a step back, to disconnect from his magical voodoo. His hand falls to his side, and the disappointment claims the luster in his eyes.

"Bita, I'm so sorry."

I know if I let him finish, to utter another word, I'll lose my conviction. I'll easily make my way back into his arms, letting him claim the other half of my heart without any

repercussions. I'll never recover.

"Stop," I demand, putting my hands up so he can't get close to me. The hurt that flashes across his expression is another wound to my dying soul. "I'm sorry Ramtin, I can't." Before he has a chance to protest, I turn and run toward the bathroom, putting distance between us. By the time I push through the doors, I'm sure my heart is no longer beating. I'm an empty vessel where Bita once lived.

Shiva is on my heels, coming in just seconds behind me. "Can we have the room for a minute, please?" she asks the two other guests washing their hands. They nod, the pity in the forced stretch of their lips easily recognizable. They hurriedly scurry out. She pushes the door shut and locks it, turning to face me. "What happened?"

"Why would you do that?" I choke back tears. "Why would you have him come?"

"Because you need to talk to him, Bita!" Her cheeks flush with frustration. "Why are you being so difficult? You're miserable. He's miserable. I can't understand why you insist on not working it out."

"There's nothing to work out."

"The hell there isn't," Shiva throws back. "You don't even know what he's thinking because you won't have a damn conversation with him."

"I don't want him to explain."

"Why not?"

"Because I don't need to have him tell me one more time why he doesn't want to have kids."

"That isn't fair, Bita."

"Why not?" I snap. She doesn't get to take his side.

"Because everyone deserves a chance."

"He had his chance. And besides, it's not like we had some stupid disagreement. He doesn't want kids. I do. What are we supposed to work out?" The tinge of desperation in my voice betrays me, letting Shiva onto my faltering strength.

"Oh, Bita," Shiva murmurs. The tenderness in her worried eyes shoves the dagger deeper into my heart.

"Don't look at me like that!" I protest. "Don't look at me like I'm some pathetic broken bird."

"First off, you're not broken. Bird or otherwise. You're my freaking hero on most days. I don't know anyone as strong as you." I give her a half-smile through the tears. "And secondly, I think it's more complicated than a simple black-and-white answer."

What is with her and Kian? Are they sharing a brain now? All this nonsense about gray zones. "Do you know something?" I ask, raising a brow. *Maybe she has information I don't.*

"No," she answers. Something in the quiver of her voice tells me she's lying. "But you won't know anything unless you talk to him." She reaches out and grabs my hand. "You can do this."

She's wrong. But suddenly there's curiosity replacing the despondency in the crevices of my will. And I know I can't stop it from propelling me forward. What if she's right? What if Ramtin has some explanation that could change everything? Shouldn't I give him the chance to say his piece? Isn't that the grownup thing to do? And God knows I'm trying to be a grownup these days.

"Bita, let's go," Shiva urges. "He loves you."

"How do you know that?"

"Because I see how he looks at you."

"How's that?"

"Like the whole world fades and nothing exists but you. There isn't a doubt in my mind that that man is hopelessly in love with you. You should hear him out, if nothing else."

"Well, then, why would he act like such an ass when he thought I might be pregnant?" I wipe the lingering tears from my cheeks, as I try to push the sprouting hope down in my chest. I look at Shiva for an answer, one that convinces me that I'm wrong about Ramtin, that there may be some other reason. Something that we can work through, because right now, that's the only thing I want.

"I don't know," she admits. "But you won't know unless you let him explain." She takes a step closer, reaching out and grabbing my hand. "Just give him a chance."

All the versions of me are dead silent in my head, leaving me to decide on my own whether I risk what little parts of my heart are left by listening to what Ramtin has to say. I know there's a chance that his explanation will only make things worse, that he'll disappoint me once again. But what if he doesn't? What if his reasons shed a little light on our dire situation? Aren't I supposed to risk it all for true love? Isn't that what all the fairy tales say?

"Okay." *Damn you, hope.*

"Good." Shiva looks confident that I'm making the right choice. I try to absorb her conviction.

We leave the bathroom hand in hand, like when we were little. Her grip around my fingers gives me the strength I need to quiet down the last of my fears, striding toward where I left Ramtin, with purpose. But when we reach the table, Kian is the only one standing there. He turns toward us with anguish in his eyes.

"He left," he explains, before I've had a chance to ask. "He said he didn't want to ruin your night more than he already had. I'm sorry, Bita."

The heartache that rams into me is so strong I reach out and grab the edge of the table trying to steady myself. Despair squeezes my organs, and I wish they'd just give out, ending my misery.

I waited too long. He's gone.

* * *

I insisted on staying at the party, making it through another hour and half before I exited the building. Shiva would have been okay with me hightailing it out of there right after the letdown of finding Ramtin had left, but I refused to accept that he'd managed to kill me once again. That, and the fact that the solitude awaiting me at home seemed unbearable. So instead, I mingled, laughed, and even danced a little. But now, as I pull into my driveway, I feel like I've been run over by a truck. Everything aches, emotionally and physically. I can hardly get out of the car and make my way over to the front door.

I'm rummaging through my purse, too exhausted to be frustrated that my keys have somehow disappeared into the leather, that I don't notice the figure sitting on the steps. When the dark shape moves, I yelp.

"I'm sorry," Ramtin says. "I didn't mean to scare you."

My heart is pounding in my ears, and I'm not entirely sure if it's because his presence on my steps scared the hell out of me or because he's actually sitting here waiting for me.

"Ramtin? What are you doing here?"

"I needed to talk to you." His frame looks small, his shoulders hunched forward in defeat, his arms resting on his knees, hands clasped tightly together. "Sorry about ruining your night."

"You didn't ruin it." I sit beside him on the step, the fight having drained out of me. His broken eyes staring down at the pavement crushes my heart. We've both seen better days, it seems.

"How was the party?"

"It was okay."

"That's good," he replies, halfheartedly.

"What did you want to talk to me about?"

I'm ready to tear off this Band-Aid. The limbo we're suddenly stuck in is something my sanity can't endure for very long.

"I hate how we left things. I wanted to explain. Nothing I said came out right."

"What is there to explain? You don't want to have kids, right?" I fight to keep the unhappiness out of my voice.

"That's not true."

"So then," I say, slowly making the horrible conclusion. "It's just me you don't want to have kids with." And here I thought the pain I was feeling couldn't get any worse. I was wrong.

"Is that what you think?" he asks, finally turning his gaze to meet mine. "You've never been more wrong." The breath catches in my throat with the agony I feel to believe him. When he wraps my hand in his, the world fades away. "You're the only one I want to have kids with."

"Well, then, why were you so upset when you thought I was pregnant?"

"I'm really sorry about how I reacted. That wasn't right," he apologizes. "But it caught me off-guard. It wasn't about you; it was about me."

"What does that mean?" *How can it not be about me?*

"It's all me," he confirms, tightening his grip on my fingers. "When Roya and I decided to get a divorce, I felt like I'd failed my girls somehow. I was hesitant about going through with it, but Roya had decided this wasn't her best life, or whatever bullshit she called it. She was being selfish. I would have stayed for my girls." He stops to push a strand of hair behind my ear. As his fingers brush my cheek, my heart stops. "It's not a baby. You know I love kids," he assures me. "But I've already failed once, and two beautiful little girls are dealing with my shortcomings. I just can't do that to another human being." His face crumbles with his pain, insecurity evident in the worry lines stretched across his forehead.

"You haven't failed," I reassure him. "When I look at Yasi and Kimiya, I see two daughters who know they're loved more than anything in the world. I see two girls that always have their dad's full attention and know that he would move mountains to keep them happy and safe. Maybe your marriage didn't work out," I add, "but you haven't, nor will you ever, fail at being a good dad." I smile as I realize he's hanging on my every word. "You're the most amazing father I've ever met. And if we were to ever have a baby and things didn't work out between us, I'd still feel lucky that he or she would have you to call Dad."

"What about my age?" he asks.

"What about it?"

"I'm so much older than you. Don't you want to be with a man your own age? I won't be one of the spunky young husbands."

Husband. I suppress a sigh. "Have you looked at yourself lately?" I laugh. "You're in better shape than most of the guys I know. I really don't think you have to worry about being spunky." I try to make light of the situation, but judging from the concern in his expression, it doesn't work.

"I appreciate the vote of confidence," he says. "But I don't think you really understand how cruel time will be. I'll age way before you're ready to. Do you want to take care of an elderly husband? Or if we have grandkids, I may never see them graduate from college or get married. You'll have to live a part of your life alone. Do you understand what that means?"

He waits patiently, allowing his words to sink in. He keeps his expression steady, no obligation or pressure evident in the tight pull of his lids. But as I stare into his seasoned eyes, I realize that no matter how much time we have together, it's worth the risk of spending the end of my life alone.

"I do understand," I answer. "And I don't care."

He pauses, taking in my features, his gaze running across the border of my jawline, the indent of my lips, the earnestness of my eyes.

"I love you so much, Bita," he whispers. He puts his arm around my waist pulling me closer to him on the step. "I can't live without you." He dips his head toward me and balances an inch away. "I'd have a million babies with you," he admits. Then he leans in and kisses me.

The feel of his mouth against mine, his hand on the small of my back, the scruffiness of his unshaven face scratching my cheek, is heaven beneath the stars. My hands find his hair, twisting into the strands, my body pushed against his chest. I want to melt into him, never to be apart again.

He pulls me to my feet and makes his way over to the door. I don't notice that he fishes for his keys and how he gets us inside. I don't know how we make it into the bedroom, but when he lays me down on the mattress, my pulse races with anticipation.

He hovers over me, staring with so much yearning, the intensity causes my skin to burn despite the absence of his touch.

"I love you," he says again.

"I love you too."

I reach up and gently outline his jaw with my finger. I run it across his lower lip and down his chin, following the trail to the center of his chest where I rest it on his wildly beating heart. He shudders beneath my touch.

"Bita," he whispers. There's a hesitation in his voice that makes my heart dance erratically in my chest.

"What is it?"

"Marry me."

My body goes still as the world moves in slow motion. *Is this really happening?* It takes me a moment to figure out I'm not dreaming, that in fact, the man of my dreams just asked me to marry him. When I don't answer right away, he chuckles. The deep baritone that rumbles through his body is the most beautiful sound I've ever heard.

I can't stop the grin from stretching widely across my face. Giddiness blooms in my chest, threatening to make me burst. "Did you just ask me to marry you?"

"Yes, I did," he answers. "So, what do you think? Do you want to be my wife?" He drops down on one elbow, so his body is pressed into mine. His mouth hovers inches away, waiting to kiss me silly.

"Yeah, I think I do."

"You sure?" he teases. He lightly brushes his lips across mine, goosebumps exploding all over my body.

"Absolutely."

EPILOGUE

"**I**s it time?" Kimiya squeals.

"No, not yet. One more minute to go." Yasi bounces on her toes with excitement.

I smile, trying to hide the anticipation consuming me. I don't want to tell them that my heart is currently tearing through my chest cavity and the air is trapped in my lungs. I can't let them see just how badly I want this. Because if we walk through the bathroom doors and we don't get the answer we're collectively praying for, it will be dishes of devastation all around. So instead, I hold onto both of my stepdaughters' hands and squeeze them reassuringly, allowing their happy jitters to wash over me.

"Time!" Yasi yells, startling me. She almost jumps into the bathroom, Kimiya closely on her heels.

I hang back, unable to make my feet obey my commands. I'm glued to the hall, terrified of the disappointment that may await me on the other side. The girls stop abruptly and turn to see what the holdup is.

"You coming?" Yasi asks. Her childlike grin contradicts her very teenage getup of tight jeans, tank top, and dark eyeliner.

Neither looks in the direction of the white plastic stick on the counter.

"We don't want to see it without you," Kimiya whines.

"Come on," Yasi pleads.

"Just give me a minute," I beg. I need to find the courage to break through the imaginary barrier stopping me.

Yasi walks back out toward me, stretching her hand out. "I'll help you," she urges. Her big, beautiful eyes remind me so much of her father's that I can't help but take her hand. Approval stretches across her face as she gently guides me into the bathroom.

"Are you ready?" Kimiya asks, grabbing hold of my other hand.

We stand in a straight line, bound by our fingers, and the new love we're building between us. As I look at each of their faces, I know I'm as ready as I'll ever be.

"Yes. Let's do this."

"Okay," Yasi says. "One...Two...Three!"

The three of us exchange one last glance between us, and peer down at the pregnancy test together, fingers intertwined, hopes melted into one. When two pink lines come into view, I stop breathing altogether.

"What does that mean?" Kimiya asks, looking back and forth between Yasi and me. "That means we're pregnant, right?"

"Yes!" Yasi screams. "We're having a baby!" She starts jumping up and down. Kimiya joins in, squealing in unison with her sister.

Their excitement would be infectious if I weren't paralyzed by disbelief. I can't stop staring at the test. *I'm pregnant. Holy hell, I'm going to have a baby.*

* * *

Three hours later, both girls are helping me set the table as we wait for Ramtin to come out of the shower. When we hear the shuffle of his feet, we force ourselves to hide our grins. Through some miracle, we manage to make it through dinner without giving away our little secret.

Every time Kimiya speaks, Yasi and I hold our breath, certain she'll show our hand. But she manages to marvelously prove us wrong. When Ramtin drops his fork onto his empty plate, the girls launch into motion, clearing the dishes without being prompted to do so. He watches them carefully, confusion and amazement evident in the curious look he's giving them.

"Who are you, and what have you done with my daughters?" he teases.

"What?" Yasi answers, giving him her teenage attitude for good measure. "We always do this."

"Maybe," he agrees, "but never this easily." He wins himself an eyeroll. But Yasi winks at me as she takes the last serving dish into the kitchen, all an act to throw him off our scent.

Kimiya turns toward me, her smile beaming with anticipation. When I nod my head, she all but bounces away from the table.

"What are you three up to?" Ramtin asks, cocking his head to the side.

I just shrug my shoulders, playing innocent. Kimiya rushes back into the room, a box materializing from behind her. She begged to be the one to execute our plan.

Even though I was sure Yasi would protest, she didn't. Instead, she sat with Kimiya, helping her expertly wrap the pretty pistachio paper. She held her index finger on the off-white bow, so her little sister could neatly tie its edges. Now she sits back in her seat and watches Kimiya put the fruits of their labor in front of their dad.

"What's this?" he asks, raising a brow.

"You'll have to open it to find out." Kimiya giggles.

She takes the seat to my left and buzzes with excitement. Yasi flashes me a knowing grin and we both inhale as Ramtin meticulously pulls on the loose ends of the bow. He moves achingly slow, suppressing his laugh, making it abundantly clear he's doing it on purpose.

Kimiya starts bouncing in her seat with enthusiasm. Yasi exhales dramatically, making her impatience with Ramtin's tactics undeniable. This wins her a teasing grin and a wink as he continues to torture us with his snail's pace.

When he's finally pulled off the last of the wrapping paper, Kimiya and Yasi straighten in their seats, trying to get a better glimpse of the gift they chose just a few hours ago, as if they have no idea what he's about to receive.

Ramtin pulls the tissue paper away, then stares down at the contents of the box, frozen. It takes him a moment, but as he reaches in and pulls out a small gray onesie with the words "World's Best Daddy" written across the front in bold navy-blue letters, understanding crosses his features.

His head snaps up and his gaze catches mine. He doesn't say a word, but his happy disbelief is blatantly obvious in the deep chocolate pools of his eyes. I can't stop the tears that spring to mine.

"We're having a baby?" he asks.

"Yes!" the girls squeal in unison.

He doesn't break eye contact when they launch themselves into his arms, both talking a mile a minute as they attempt to express how ecstatic they are. When a smile of pure joy stretches across his face, the tears roll down my cheeks. He watches me intently as I lean back in my chair and protectively lay a hand across my nonexistent belly.

He makes his way over to my side of the table, reaching out his big broad hand to find my smaller one. He intertwines our fingers then gently rests his palm on my stomach.

"We're having a baby?"

"Yes, we are."

He guides me to my feet. "We're having a baby," he repeats, then wraps his arms around my waist, pressing his body into mine. The feel of his strong, protective embrace causes a frenzy of wings to flap uncontrollably in my chest. He lightly kisses the crown of my head and begins swaying slowly from side to side, as if we're dancing to a song only he can hear.

"Are you happy?" I ask. My voice breaks, a small portion of me still terrified that he really doesn't want any more kids.

"Absolutely," he whispers in my ear. Relief floods through me and I melt into him.

Kimiya and Yasi come up beside us, wrapping their arms tightly around our waists. As Rantim stares at me above their heads, tears shining in his eyes, I know with certainty that my life is exactly as it should be.

THE END

Thank you for reading! Did you enjoy?

Please Add Your Review! And don't miss more romance novels like, BETTER TOGETHER. Turn the page for a sneak peek!

"No way am I going in there." Harper Bright took a second look at the yawning black hole in the mountain in front of her and crossed her arms over her chest. She didn't need her doctorate degree to know this was a bad idea.

"Did you know this tunnel was on Hitler's charts during World War II? If he ever made it stateside, it was one of the places he planned to bomb." Wyatt Fernandez planted his feet and put his hands on his hips. His dimples flashed but he spoke in the tone of voice that said, "I hear you, but I'm ignoring you".

He used the same tone every time he dragged Harper on some crazy adventure or another.

She walked toward the openmouthed hole. Despite her family having owned the ground around the tunnel all her life, she hadn't known about this small spot in Central Pennsylvania being on Hitler's map.

The looming mountain that shot up around the ravenous cavity blocked the sunlight. Leafy green trees waved in the warm June breeze. Harper squinted up. "You know, someday, we really ought to start acting like the mature adults we are."

"Gimme a break, Harper. The only time you ever spend two

seconds not acting like an adult is when I strong arm you into it. Like now. This is going to be fun." Wyatt flashed that irresistible dimple and his brown eyes twinkled. Harper wasn't exactly short, but she still had to crane her neck to look at him as he walked beside her. His lanky frame had filled out in the decade since high school. Actually, now that she thought about it, he'd filled out very nicely. Broad chest, wide shoulders, and long, muscular legs. A flare of heat unfurled in her stomach. She straightened her spine. This was Wyatt. Her best friend.

They reached the orifice of the mountain. Cool air blew from its depths. It smelled heavy and sweet, like rotting soil. Their next steps took them inside. The hair on the back of Harper's neck poked straight out. She scooted closer to Wyatt.

"I'm not seeing the 'fun' part." Her voice echoed off the cavernous walls. Water dripped hollowly, echoing in the blackness.

Wyatt kept walking. "This isn't supposed to be fun. It's research. Do you want to find it or not?"

Harper bumped Wyatt's arm with her shoulder. "You know I do."

She wanted to see if the old stories were true, but couldn't help shivering as she looked around at the stone walls arching above. The farther in they walked, the darker it got. At this point, she could barely see Wyatt's outline. She pushed back the fear threatening to break loose in her head. It wasn't that walking in the tunnel was particularly dangerous. It was more the idea of the dark unknown and being trapped in a small space with an angry locomotive.

As if Wyatt could read her mind, he said, "There isn't any danger if a train would actually go through while we're in here. Although, I have heard that there could be a bit of air suction."

She planted her feet. "What?"

"Kidding." He pulled on her arm. "Come on."

She started walking again. Slowly. "What did you mean by air suction?" Wyatt had always been better with hard science. All she'd cared about was finding the family heirloom that her great-great grandmother had told her was hidden in the deepest depths.

Wyatt tapped her head with the hand that wasn't dragging her toward the tunnel. "Well, since you're the brain in this relationship..."

She swatted his hand and continued to drag her feet, even though she'd already decided to go along with his nutty scheme, the way she always did. After all, not only did she want to find the ring, but this could be the last time Wyatt and she went on an adventure together. She'd gotten the call yesterday that her tenure vote was scheduled for the end of summer. It was the one last thing she had to cross off the list of career goals she'd made the day she had graduated from high school.

"Quit it. You're smarter than me, and we both know it. I just happen to be able to stay in one place long enough to get a degree." It wasn't that she was so smart. She was simply willing to work hard. Plus, she liked to study. She'd enjoyed every second of the last ten years. Which led her to the vexatious question that had plagued her since the phone call: *what now?*

"Ouch." Wyatt placed a hand over his heart.

She shrugged. Too often she'd wondered that maybe what she'd been working toward all this time wasn't what she really wanted anymore. More likely she had become overly comfortable with achieving her goals, ticking each accomplishment off of her internal checklist. "It's true."

"Yeah, well, you had a nice, secure home all your life."

And he hadn't. Never really knowing or being wanted by his father, losing his mother in a tragic skiing accident, being sent to live with an uncle he barely knew. Of course, if he hadn't come to live with the man her mother eventually married, she would never have gotten to know him. She bit her lip. "I'm sorry."

"Hey, not a problem. I'll only rub it in if you change your mind and turn around."

They walked far enough into the tunnel that the light behind them faded, and Harper could no longer see the road under her feet. Dread balled and rolled in the pit of her stomach. She reached for Wyatt. Big and strong with rough calluses, his hand enfolded hers with an ease born of familiarity.

How could she have forgotten how easily Wyatt's touch could calm her? All the numerous phone conversations and thousands of text messages couldn't replicate the comfort of his touch. The miles between them had always multiplied Harper's anxiety. The pictures he sent hadn't helped. Standing at the top of some snow-covered mountain with only clouds and sky in the background, or his arms outstretched, moments before he leapt from a who-knows-how-high cliff with only a thin bundle—hopefully a parachute—strapped to his back. Of course, she wasn't sure which was worse, the pictures, or the times when she didn't hear from him for days. He always warned her when he might be adventuring out of service areas, but that was one instance when knowledge wasn't power, as her ragged bloody nails could testify.

"Do you think we're halfway?" she asked.

"Why are you whispering?"

She shivered—she hadn't noticed she was whispering. "Just in case there's a bear hibernating in one of those alcoves you talked about."

"It's June."

"Maybe it's waking up late this year." Even to her ears it sounded asinine. Her cheeks heated. She looked over, but they were so deep in the mountain that she couldn't see a thing. The darkness hid her flush. Lifting her chin, she tried to focus on the stories she'd heard as a child. If they found what they were looking for, it would be worth facing her fear.

"I can't believe someone has actually hired you to teach college students." He squeezed her hand, and she didn't need a light to know he smiled beside her.

"I revert to my inner child when I'm scared spitless."

Wyatt activated his cell phone light. "There." He pointed it at the wall. Sure enough, just ahead an arched area was chiseled into the side of mountain. "Maybe three feet deep, three feet long and," he looked up, "seven or so feet high. We'd both fit in there easy."

"Us and the serial killer that eludes the cops by hiding in here." She tugged on his hand. "Come on. Faster."

"Didn't you ever hear you gotta enjoy the journey?" Harper could hear the grin in Wyatt's voice, but he did speed up a notch. For her. Heck, this was child's play compared to the stuff he normally did.

But it was Wyatt, and she didn't have to pretend to be brave. "I'll enjoy it once we're out of here."

"It'll be over then." He chuckled. "Oh, except we have to walk back through."

She stopped so fast her feet probably left skid marks. But she wouldn't know since it was darker than sin, and she couldn't see a blasted thing except for the far tunnel opening which didn't seem to be getting any closer.

"We only have to go to the middle hidey hole. That's where it's supposed to be. No one said anything about walking through." Fear had turned her backbone into an icicle. "I know you're an adrenaline junkie, but I'm allergic to the stuff."

Wyatt snorted. "If it weren't for me, you'd be moldering under your books and lab rats. How many times have you left the state?"

"Three. And it was three too many. I like being home. I like moldering." She kept her eyes fastened to the circle of light on the ground from Wyatt's cell phone until he put it away.

"I like being home, too. But being home is sweeter after you've left it for a while." His thumb moved lightly over her knuckles.

A little of her tension eased. "I always assumed you had itchy feet like your mom."

"A little, I guess."

"If that's not it, why not come home? You know Fink and my mom would love to have you back helping out on the farm." She'd love to have him back, too. Gosh, she missed him. She hadn't realized how much.

Even though he'd been away more than home the last few years, she still considered him her best friend. They had always told each other everything.

Well, except anything that even hinted of romance. Growing up, she'd always been very aware that her mother had gotten pregnant with her at fourteen. Harper had determined not to go down the same path, closing herself off to the very idea of boys or boyfriends. Studying instead of dating. She supposed, at twenty-eight, it was probably okay to crack that protective shell.

"Come on, Pickles. We're almost half-way. The next hidey-hole is probably close." His deep voice rumbled above her.

She smiled at the nickname he had gifted her with years ago.

Light cut through the darkness parallel to the ground—the wrong angle for Wyatt's cell phone—just before he tensed beside her. The rumble in the air and the vibration under her feet confirmed what her brain had suspected. She turned to be sure. The entire mouth of the tunnel was blocked out by the massive shape of a train engine. Like a flesh-eating bacteria, magnified, with teeth bared, it bore down on them.

Acid shards cut through her trembling body. She barely felt Wyatt yanking on her arm. She couldn't get her feet to move. The engine powered closer like a black avalanche, chewing up the distance between them.

He swept her up in his arms and jogged the two steps to the nook, flattening himself against the side wall so his back was toward the train. The roar of the engine and the squeal of metal on steel reverberated throughout the stone walls. The vibration seemed to be alive, monstrous, so close and big and loud she could almost see it. She pulled her body into a ball and pressed against him. She wrapped her arms around his head, wanting to protect him, too.

Her breath came in short gasps. Panic rolled through her like a bowling ball heading toward the king pin.

She closed her eyes tight, until it was only Wyatt's solid, comforting warmth pressing into her and the deafening noise all around. He cradled her and bent over slightly. The tangy, heavy stench of diesel exhaust filled the air around them, burning Harper's nose.

Eventually the engine noise faded away and, although the train was still loud, the cars passing had a more rhythmic feel. Loud clack-clack, then fading out before coming back combined with the occasional earsplitting screech of metal on metal.

Wyatt's stubble rubbed her cheek. She closed her eyes and moved her cheek back over his. Her chest tingled. She froze and her eyes snapped open. This was Wyatt. Her best friend. She would not allow their friendship to be ruined because she all of a sudden had some wild ribbon of desire winding through her. No matter how delicious it was.

His breath warmed her ear as he said, "Now we know there's no air suction."

"I'm going to poison the next meal I make you," she hissed into his neck, only half-joking.

"I've heard that before." His heart beat steady and strong against her. The dratted man wasn't even scared.

The last of the cars went by. The noise faded.

She loosened her arms from around his head. She didn't know what she was trying to protect him from anyway.

It was probably time to remember she was a grown-up. A professor up for tenure vote at the end of the summer. But Wyatt's warmth and strength were alluring. She didn't want to pull away from the hardness of his chest or lose the comfort of his touch. But she couldn't let him stand here holding her forever.

"Okay, put me down." She lifted her head and smacked his shoulder lightly, pretending she hadn't been clutching him like two oxygen atoms on a hydrogen, and praying her knees wouldn't buckle when he complied.

She wiggled to prompt him to move, but a new sound echoed in the darkness and she froze. A hiss. Followed by a rattle.

"Holy crap." Her arms tightened around Wyatt's neck. "Is that what I think it is?"

"Yeah. Someone's practicing the maracas." She could feel his head tilt in the darkness. "They're pretty good."

Her teeth rattled together, but she snorted a laugh. "That's a rattlesnake. It sounds close."

"I don't think we need to worry. I thought it was a stick when I first stepped on it, but sticks don't typically wrap themselves around your leg."

Chills raced up Harper's spine. Her mouth opened, but it took a minute to make her voice work. "You're standing on the snake?"

"Yes, ma'am."

The sound like stones shaking in a tin can echoed throughout the tunnel again.

She ignored the note of sarcasm in his voice. "What are we going to do?"

"You're the one with the doctorate. How about I keep standing on the snake while you think?"

Her throat slammed shut. She struggled to swallow. "I study nutrition. In a lab. That's what the doctorate is for. Food."

"Branch out a little."

Despite Harper's all-encompassing fear, she smiled. "Okay." She took a deep breath. If he wasn't worried, if he thought it was funny, well, she could do humor, too. "I'm thinking about white sandy beaches, relaxing waves, warm sun..."

"Try again."

She grinned—still petrified, but Wyatt exuded calm. "Hey, that was helping."

He snorted.

Ideas were not exactly filling her mind. Her brain had diverted all her blood flow to the areas that made her want to pee and run at the same time. She went with the only plan she could think of. "How about I grab your cell phone out of your pocket. I'll shine the flashlight down at your feet..."

"Um, close your eyes while you do it, just in case..."

Harper twisted gingerly in his arms and felt for the phone attached to his belt, not wanting to make him lose his balance, although he seemed rock solid. Funny, because she still pictured Wyatt as a gangly teen instead of the unflappable man holding her in his arms and not even breathing hard. "Just in case what?"

Silence.

"Wyatt. Is there something you're not telling me?"

"Not really."

Not really? That meant there was something. What could be worse than a rattle snake? "If there was a bear in this hidey hole, I'd have figured it out by now."

"I'm sure you would have, Pickles." He shifted ever so slightly. "Would you just shine the light down?"

She paused with the phone in her shaking hand. "What does 'not really' mean? You're standing on the snake, right?"

"One of them."

"Holy crap. Holy crap. Holy crap."

He gave her the password to his phone. She pulled up the flashlight app with shaking fingers. Something caught her eye in a crack in the stone behind Wyatt's head. Her racing heart jumped. She squinted to see more clearly. She'd forgotten the reason they were in the tunnel in the first place.

"Harper? Tell me you're not playing Candy Crush."

"Uh. No. Of course not." She juggled the phone to her other hand. Once they got the snake figured out, she could examine the crack more closely. There was definitely something there. Faded blue fabric, maybe?

She shone the light at the ground, keeping her eyes trained on the wall. Now that she knew something was there, she could see the shadow that marked the spot.

Wyatt shuddered. "Eh, I was wrong."

"Thank God." Cool relief flooded her. Her fingers lifted and skimmed the smooth surface of the stone.

"There's three."

She tensed.

Then yelped.

She dropped his phone.

Wyatt jerked.

With her free hand, she slapped at the wall. A small object landed in her palm.

* * *

Grab your copy of BETTER TOGETHER available now. Sign up for the City Owl Press newsletter to receive notice of all book releases!

Love kindles when a fake engagement brings best friends together.

World Champion snowboarder, Wyatt Fernandez, should be hitting the slopes in the Andes and spending his days teaching as the new ski instructor. But an emergency means he's heading off the family's tree farm with his best friend, Harper. She's too busy with her books and earning tenure to notice his hopes for more than friendship.

Homebody and nutritionist, Dr. Harper Bright, must let go of her coveted summer research position so she can help on the tree farm...with Wyatt. He might push past her comfort zone, but he has always "gotten" her. She doesn't want to scare off her best friend just because he is suddenly far more interesting than the nutritional benefits of broccoli. In order to keep their friendship intact, Harper has to pretend she is not infatuated with her best friend.

When Wyatt names Harper as his fiancé to appease his father and prevent returning to Chile early, he never dreams Harper might actually have to play the part. Wyatt wants more than a reluctant fake fiancé. And he has one last summer to convince Harper that they're better together.

* * *

All reviews are **welcome** and **appreciated**. Please consider leaving one on your favorite social media and book buying sites.

For books in the world of romance and speculative fiction that embody Innovation, Creativity, and Affordability, check out City Owl Press at www.cityowlpress.com.

ACKNOWLEDGMENTS

FORBIDDEN BY TIME is bittersweet for me because it signifies the end of my Forbidden Love series. It both overwhelms me with the excitement of knowing that I've *actually* written a three-part romance, but also with a sadness that my journey with these characters, and their stories, has come to an end. It's strange how attached I've gotten to them despite their fictional nature. But when you're immersed in a world for so many years, it's hard to not feel as if they truly exist. Even if it's only in your mind.

If someone would have asked me a few years back if I could have predicted any of this, I'd have said no. I hadn't thought to see "author" in my future because I still hadn't given myself the right to dream. But sometimes, the unexpected opens up closed doors that set you free. Writing has given me wings. With each set of author copies that make it to my door, I still stand in disbelief that my name is scrawled across their covers. But I guess that's what dreams are: surreal, unbelievable, magical.

I've been fortunate to be surrounded by a group of amazing, confident, fierce women throughout this journey. They've always been my pillars, encouraging me to keep going, even when I can't understand why I would want to. They've had faith in me where I lacked it, and determination when I needed it. Without them, my writing, and my sanity, would not be the same. I've thanked them many times before, but it will never be enough. So, to the lovely humans that have held my hand so steadfastly throughout these years: Ann, Leslie, Melissa, Michelle, thank you from the bottom of my heart.

Yelena, thank you for all the time and work you put into Forbidden by Time. I'm so grateful that you agreed to jump in on this project when you did. Despite this being the third book, I have learned so much from you and am definitely a better writer for it. I hope this isn't the end of the road for us.

To my City Owl fam, you all rock and are amazing! I couldn't ask for a better tribe.

I also need to take a moment to thank my mother-in-law, Minoo. She allowed me to take up a morning brunch to interview her on the details of their escape from Iran so that I could weave it into Forbidden by Time, allowing Ramtin to claim it as his own. She combed through her memories of this difficult experience, and through uncontrollable tears, gave me everything I asked for. Thank you for sharing this part of your life and history with me. I love you.

Mike, thanks for not allowing me to give up. When the fear of how my novels would be perceived by those around us made me want to stop, you pushed me to keep going, always encouraging me to be true to the stories of my heart. You helped give me the confidence I needed to make this happen. I love you.

To my readers, without you, none of this would be possible. Writing novels is just the beginning. Without you to pick them up, read them, get lost in them, feel every emotion, tear, injustice with my characters, it would mean nothing. I'm grateful for being given the opportunity to share my books with you. I hope you've enjoyed going on this journey with me. And I hope I've shared pieces of my culture with you that you hadn't known. With each Iranian woman I created, I wanted to show the parts of being Persian that the world doesn't always see. There is beauty, peace, love, and family, woven deeply in my culture. All you have to do is open your hearts and take a look. I hope the Forbidden Love series has helped you do that.

Lastly, to my boys who get a tribute in every acknowledgment. Life isn't always fabulous and sometimes it's just plain hard. But *always* be true to yourselves. Dream big, reach for the stars, and leave your footprint behind. Find ways to allow your soul to soar across the sky in a trail of glitter and starlight. And always, *always*, find the joy. I love you two more than there are words in every language of the world. You are amazing. You are kind. You are everything I dreamed for, and perfect just the way you are. You are my little slices of heaven...

ABOUT THE AUTHOR

NEGEEN PAPEHN was born and raised in southern California, where she currently lives with her husband and two rambunctious boys. She wasn't always a writer. A graduate of USC dental school, Negeen spends half of her week with patients and the other half in front of her laptop. In the little time she finds in between, she loves to play with her boys, go wine tasting with her friends, throw parties, and relax with her family.

Website: www.negeenpapehn.com

Twitter: twitter.com/NegeenPapehn

Facebook: www.facebook.com/NegeenPapehn/

Instagram: www.instagram.com/NegeenPapehn/

ABOUT THE PUBLISHER

City Owl Press is a cutting edge indie publishing company, bringing the world of romance and speculative fiction to discerning readers.

www.cityowlpress.com

Made in the USA
San Bernardino, CA
03 July 2019